I've travelled the world twice over,
Met the famous: saints and sinners,
Poets and artists, kings and queens,
Old stars and hopeful beginners,
I've been where no-one's been before,
Learned secrets from writers and cooks
All with one library ticket
To the wonderful world of books.

© JANICE JAMES.

SOPHIE IS GONE

Called to the murder of a senior surgeon in the grounds of a country hospital, John Charter discovers that his ex-wife, Sophie, is involved in the case. Then she disappears. He ought to retire from the investigation, but he persuades the Assistant Chief Constable to give him forty-eight hours to land his chief suspect. The hospital staff close ranks and Charter wrestles with rumours of medical malpractice by young doctors and of fierce rivalries between colleagues. He works at breakneck speed in the fear that he may never find Sophie alive.

Books by Anne Fleming
in the Ulverscroft Large Print Series:

THERE GOES CHARLIE

ANNE FLEMING

SOPHIE IS GONE

Complete and Unabridged

ULVERSCROFT
Leicester

First published in Great Britain in 1994 by
Robert Hale Limited
London

First Large Print Edition
published 1996
by arrangement with
Robert Hale Limited
London

British Library CIP Data

Fleming, Anne
    Sophie is gone.—Large print ed.—
Ulverscroft large print series: mystery
1. English fiction—20th century
I. Title
823.9′14 [F]

ISBN 0–7089–3538–9

Published by
F. A. Thorpe (Publishing) Ltd.
Anstey, Leicestershire

Set by Words & Graphics Ltd.
Anstey, Leicestershire
Printed and bound in Great Britain by
T. J. Press (Padstow) Ltd., Padstow, Cornwall

This book is printed on acid-free paper

1

Rope Walk

THE news of the murder at St Christopher's, Stumpington, came at a bad moment for John Charter. Sophie was with him in the small house he'd bought for himself at Penchester now, almost a year after the divorce. He wanted her to stay so badly that he was saying all the wrong things. And then came the telephone call and the instant summons and the familiar look he'd always seen on Sophie's face on such occasions when she'd still been married to him — a mixture of anger and frustration turning to reluctant resignation. This time the resignation was missing. Before he could put out a hand to stop her she had grabbed at her raincoat and camera bag and walked out of the house shutting the door behind her with a snap.

When the bell had rung ten minutes

earlier he'd thought it must be a friend or a colleague. There she was at the foot of the steps looking up at him, her mackintosh slung carelessly over her shoulders, her wet, light-blonde hair curling wildly over her forehead, a half smile on her face and a question in her eyes.

He went down to her in one leap and brought her up and in, an arm round her waist. His wide exulting welcoming smile brought a reluctant answering smile from Sophie. Then her eyes went round the room he'd made out of three-ground-floor boxes. She walked round looking at china, touching a vase, smiling at the Daumier cartoon and stopping at an array of decanters on the painted chest beside the Aga.

"Give me a drink, John," she said, and sank on to a leather armchair rather suddenly as if her body had folded in the middle. Then he knew that something was wrong and what she had come for was help. This pleased him but at the same time he felt a faint stirring of apprehension.

"Children all right?" he asked as

carelessly as he could, pouring sherry for her.

"No," she said and he turned sharply. "No, no, the children are fine. No sherry. Whisky."

He handed it to her and she drank a good half of it straight off and set it down.

He sat near her on the piano stool and raised his own glass to her.

"I'm glad you came, Sophie. What's the matter?"

"How do you know anything's the matter? No, don't answer that. You always did. It used to drive me mad."

"Come on, Sophie. You didn't come for my beautiful blue eyes."

"It's nothing important. Nothing really bad. I've just done something embarrassing and careless and I've got to make it all right and I don't know how."

"I see. And I might know how?"

"You always do." There was resentment in the way she said it. That was his Sophie. Asking for help with one hand and hating him for giving it with the other. It didn't matter what you did you couldn't get it right with Sophie.

3

"Very well," he said. "What do you want me to do?"

She sipped her drink and looked at him speculatively over the rim of her glass.

"Well," she said, "it's Oscar Hay."

"Oscar Hay? What on earth has Oscar Hay got to do with you?"

"He seems to think he's in love with me."

"Oh, he does, does he? What should I say? Congratulations?" He got up and prowled about the room.

"I knew you'd be annoyed."

He turned on her. "I'm not annoyed. I'm worried for you. Honestly, Sophie, you ought not to be allowed out on your own. A man in his position. What's the point?"

"Since you are a detective you ought to try to listen to what people say. I didn't say I was in love with Oscar Hay."

"Then what are we talking about?"

"I had to photograph him at the House of Commons for *The Prattler*. He kept me waiting for hours. A division or something came up. It got rather late so he took me out to dinner. We got on quite well."

4

"Good God, Sophie, you must have known that could only end in tears."

"Whose tears? I went out to dinner with him a few times. His wife has a very public boyfriend so I didn't see any harm in it. He's rather nice. Not a bit prospective cabinet minister. Well, if you want to know. It was very very stupid of me. I spent the night with him. I didn't mean to but he looked at me across the table and he said, 'You're magic'. It's awfully difficult not to fall a little bit in love with someone who tells you you're magic even if you know he's being absurd. And you know me and champagne. We drank more than a bottle between us. So I ended up in bed with him at Bray."

She looked at him rather defiantly and he swallowed hard and stretched out to take her hand.

"I hate to hear that," he said. "But I know it's none of my business. You're so funny, Sophie! In bed with him at Bray! Go on."

"Well," she said, "you must admit. Almost a cabinet minister. He's only thirty-nine."

"But you aren't in love with him?"

"Honestly, John, when do you imagine I'd find the time? And anyway, he's much too interested in Oscar Hay."

"So it ended in tears for him?"

"It ended in a stream of passionate love letters. I wouldn't have thought he had it in him. He went completely overboard. Couldn't believe I'm much too busy to be bothered with that sort of thing."

"He didn't offer to leave his wife?"

"No, of course not."

"Blast him!"

"Well you could hardly expect him to. Don't get so worked up about it, John. I'm an expert on that sort of situation. If I make a friend you can be quite sure her husband will start the slow gavotte in my direction and sometimes not so blamed slow either. They've no intention of leaving their wives but the wives are always afraid they might. Poor dears. They all seem to be under the impression that their husbands are totally irresistible. Rather touching really."

She cast him a sideways glance and began to laugh. Charter burst out laughing, leaned over and kissed her cheek. "I'm glad you don't find them irresistible," he said.

She stiffened immediately. "What's it bloody got to do with you?"

"Only this. I want you back one day and a new husband would be an inconvenience."

Sophie looked at him crossly and decided to ignore this remark.

"John," she said, "someone's got hold of one of the letters."

"Oscar Hay's?"

"Yes."

"Who?"

"A friend of mine. I was playing squash with him and he lent me his anorak. I left the letter in the pocket by mistake."

"And this character read it?"

"Yes, I'm afraid so. He went completely berserk."

"Is he in love with you himself?"

"No, not in the least. But he thinks it's conduct unbecoming a future cabinet minister. He thinks the Prime Minister ought to see it."

"He can't do that. That's conduct unbecoming if anything is. Is he **going** to blackmail the man?"

7

"Oh no. He couldn't do that. He's one of the surgeons at St Christopher's."

"It sounds to me as if he's barking mad. Either that or he's got to be in love with you himself."

"I assure you he's not. I suppose he just thinks a future cabinet minister ought to have better morals. He's very keen on the family. Perhaps because they haven't any children. Only goats."

"Goats?"

"His wife keeps goats. They have initialled rugs like show horses and she and the au pair girl take them all over the country competing."

"Poor chap."

"He spends most of his time at the hospital. He's a marvellous brain surgeon. God, I'd hate it if the Press got hold of that letter."

"He'd hardly give it to the Press."

"No, I suppose not. But I couldn't count on it."

"He sounds a blister."

"He's not. I'm rather fond of him. But every so often he gets plastered and then he tends to fly off the handle."

"How very reassuring for his patients."

"It's only because he's unhappy. And he's a brilliant surgeon. He saves people who've been completely given up."

"So what do you want me to do?"

"Could you talk to him? Make him give the letter back. I don't want to have to tell Oscar I was so careless and I don't particularly want to be the one to ruin his beastly career."

"No," he said, "I do agree with that."

"Someone's going to ruin it but not your wife," said Sophie.

"Come on, Sophie. That's not what I said. You know I didn't mean that."

"Oh yes you bloody did."

He sat down on the arm of her chair and took her hand. "Sophie, love," he said. "You never used to drink neat whisky. What's the matter?"

"I've told you."

"That's nothing to worry about. I'll deal with this sanctimonious medical man. Are you sure you and Robert and India are all right?"

"I've told you we are."

"Then you won't even think about coming back?"

"No, I won't."

It was then that the telephone rang. And no sooner had he said 'I'll be there in twenty minutes', than he heard the door shut and Sophie was gone. He decided against going after her, picked up his mackintosh and an ancient tweed hat and let himself out of the house.

2

St Christopher's

AT first they'd thought it was a tramp, this body lying in the dark leafy lane which led from the back courtyard of St Christopher's Hospital to the three big private houses belonging to the hospital. He'd been dressed in sweater and flannels and shabby trainers now soaking wet and, at close quarters, he gave off a faint stale smell of alcohol. It was only when the au pair girl who'd found him quietened down and became coherent that they realized that she knew who it was. That perhaps explained the incessant high pitched screaming in a girl who looked too sensible for hysterics.

By the time Detective Chief Superintendent John Charter arrived from Penchester they'd got her up to the house and, of all people, the victim's wife, was feeding her hot glucose drinks. Overalled scene-of-crime men were still busy about the body, the lane was cordoned off and a police constable stood on guard at the archway leading from the lane to the back courtyard of the hospital through which Charter had come.

The police surgeon, swathed in oilskins, came to meet him in the glare from the mobile lighting system which picked out the fine rain blowing away into the darkness in glittering gusts.

"You can take him away as soon as they've finished," he said. "Harvey Knott has had a look and it's all quite straightforward. The blunt instrument's lying there beside him covered in blood and tissue. Hasn't been dead much over an hour. They'll tell you more when they've had him on the table. I'm off now."

"Thank you, Dickie."

"But I have to say that I do rather resent people knocking off my colleagues."

"Ah," said Charter, "a colleague? Then we'd better get on with it, hadn't we?"

Dickie Lambert marched away to his car and Detective Sergeant Cobbold appeared out of the shadows. They smiled broadly at each other as they shook hands and Charter said, "Glad to see you, Derek. And CID now."

"Thanks to you, sir," said the sergeant.

"Well?"

"It's a professor, sir. A top surgeon from this hospital. Professor Gurth Tancred."

"Who identified the body?"

"A Miss Silke von Treiben. A German girl who works for the Tancreds. That's their house over there with all the lights on behind the chestnut trees. It's the nearest to the hospital of the three houses in the lane. They're all attached to the hospital and the lane's a cul-de-sac. No one else uses it."

"Who lives in the second and the third?"

"A Miss Fisher who's a top nursing officer in the second and a Mr Jackson of the hospital administration in the third. It's the biggest."

"Naturally."

The photographers were packing up.

"There's not much to go on, sir," said the sergeant. "Except this."

Two scene-of-crime men in blue overalls were leaning lovingly over a smeared imprint at the side of the lane. It was

13

a made-up lane but there were patches of mud along the edges where the fence cut the lane off from the surrounding parkland. One of the men said, "It's some sort of boot, sir, if it's not trainers. Rubber soles with indentations. Easy to identify, but probably thousands of them about. Not all that accurate unfortunately as to shoe size."

Cobbold showed Charter the bloodstains under the protecting tent.

"Here's where he was hit, sir. Large amounts of blood. He must have been covered with it. And we think he tried to drag the body away. Here he stops and drops it. Someone came this way and frightened him off. We think it was the girl who found him."

"Trying to get him to one of the houses or to the trees a little further on. It wouldn't be too difficult to get the body through the fence there. The wires are almost touching the ground. It would have delayed discovery of the body."

"And then the girl turned up. Bad luck for him."

"Looks like unpremeditated on the face of it."

"Yes, sir. The weapon came out of the fence. It's one of the uprights. They're all falling down. Easy enough to pull it out."

"It's done a lot of damage," said Charter, examining the head wound with distaste. "Nothing much here for the lab. A sudden blow from behind. Looks like being a difficult one. We'll have to hope the murderer knew the victim."

He stood up.

"Right, lads," he said. "Briefing at the station as soon as may be. No one goes home until we've had the PM report. Now where's the DI?"

"Detective Inspector Longfield was planning to attend the PM while waiting for your arrival, sir. Perhaps you'll want to join him there? He's sealed off the hospital while we search the grounds and he's getting all the staff and able-bodied patients screened. There's a temporary incident room near the front entrance on the ground floor. Would you like me to show you?"

"We'll just call at the Tancred house first," said Charter and the sergeant smiled reminiscently and followed his superior along the lane. The body, its hands and head enclosed in plastic, was zipped into its black bag, strapped down and wheeled away.

"This man," said Charter. "This colleague of Dickie Lambert's. He doesn't happen to be a neurosurgeon, does he?"

"A brain surgeon, sir? Yes, that's just what he is. It seems a terrible waste. Is it significant?"

"I don't know, Derek."

They walked up to the handsome Georgian house, greeted the constable standing patiently at the door, his coat collar turned up against the rain, and rang the bell. The door was slightly ajar and when no one answered the bell they pushed it open and looked into a beautifully proportioned entrance hall floored in black and white squares. In a corner stood a circular carved coatstand. Various mackintoshes and anoraks, tweed hats and caps hung on this. Below was an untidy array of wellington boots, tennis and squash racquets. As Charter saw these his eyes went bleak. It looked as if Professor Tancred might conceivably be Sophie's sanctimonious medical man.

16

If so, he ought to take himself off the case at once.

A woman came out of the room on the right.

"Police?" she asked as she saw them standing there.

Charter went forward. "Yes, ma'am," he said. "Detective Chief Superintendent John Charter and Sergeant Cobbold. Mrs Tancred?"

"Yes. I'm Myra Tancred." She looked quite composed. A broad-shouldered woman wearing an Arran sweater and tweed slacks. Her hair was tied back and pinned up in a bun. Her face was high cheek-boned and sharp-chinned. Her eyes were very bright blue. At present they were wide open and almost unblinking.

She turned and led the way into the drawing-room which was large and rose-coloured and luxuriously carpeted and curtained. A girl was sitting on the floor huddled up close to the blazing log fire clutching a blanket round her shoulders. Three empty mugs stood in the hearth.

"This is Fraulein von Treiben who helps me with the chores. She found my husband. She was in shock when they

17

brought her home. I think she's better now."

She went to Silke and pressed her shoulder with a reassuring hand then turned rather stiffly to seat herself near the fire and waved them to a large chesterfield. She looked down at Silke and a strange smile came over her face which seemed to express detached and distant tenderness reminding Charter of the half smile on the face of an archaic Greek statue. Sitting very upright on the edge of her chair she went on talking fast in a high toneless voice, her eyes fixed on the girl's face.

"It was quite terrible for Silke because she was in love with my husband. He needed these little affairs from time to time and I didn't mind very much because he kept them quite secret and they never lasted very long. The girl before Silke was one of the doctors at the hospital. She took it very well when he ditched her. She was more sophisticated than Silke. Older, too. Silke is only eighteen, and quite naive in some ways. She came to me for comfort when Gurth got tired of her. Why do you think

Gurth was killed? Who could have done it? Was it just a tramp or a mugger, do you think? Or was it to do with his little affairs? I expect they meant more to the girls than they did to him. Do you think that might be the explanation?" She asked the question politely and quite without emotion, as if gossiping over the tea cups. And still she smiled on Silke.

Charter got up. "Mrs Tancred," he said gently, "have you anyone in the house to look after you? You're in shock yourself, you know. Can we telephone your doctor?"

She looked up at him and tears began to pour down her cheeks. She began to utter little moans.

Silke jumped up and ran to her. "I'll look after her," she said. "I'll put her to bed. You call the doctor. The number's on the pad."

The sergeant went to the telephone and Charter opened the door for the two women. They went into the hall and walked very slowly up the stairs, their arms round each other. The moans died away and a door shut softly.

Charter and Cobbold left the house

and walked down the lane to the hospital. Charter was frowning and Cobbold stole a look at him and offered no comment. The rain had stopped. Drops fell from the leaves and twigs and branches and plopped on the tarmac. Charter was hurriedly trying to sort out in his mind all the possibilities inherent in the awful likelihood that Sophie was involved in all this and what he ought to do if she was. There was no proof that Professor Tancred was the man who had played squash with Sophie and taken the letter, but was there more than one squash-playing neurosurgeon at St Christopher's? He must find out the name from Sophie as soon as he could. How like her to have asked him to deal with the problem and then to walk out leaving him without a name or an address. He had been quite right to tell her that she shouldn't be allowed out alone. Yet there she was, in sole charge of Robert and India. Getting the three of them back was his most urgent problem and if he wasn't careful his worry over this would end up by losing him his job.

How likely was it that Professor

Tancred was Sophie's brain surgeon, this character who played squash, read other people's letters and set himself up as judge of other people's morals? In view of the trainers he was wearing at the time of his death it seemed likely that Tancred was the owner of the squash racquets at the house. So he was a squash player. He was also a surgeon and a neurosurgeon into the bargain. But there the comparison broke down. Sophie's friend took a high moral tone. Mrs Tancred's husband, on the other hand, had seduced a young girl under his own roof. Surely the man must see that this was at least as immoral as Oscar Hay's extra-marital affairs. But Charter had been long enough in the business of dealing with human motives to know that in this area the rules of logic don't apply. And it was quite on the cards that Silke had made all the running with Tancred herself. A girl could well have become even a mini-Messalina in these days by the time she was eighteen.

"Sergeant," he said. "You used to be rural sergeant. How likely do you think it is that Mrs Tancred keeps goats?"

The sergeant looked at him in surprise, and said, "Well, sir, I did wonder what sort of livestock they had out the back. There was a distinct smell of animal on her clothes and I don't know whether you noticed the straw in her hair. Is it important?"

"An idle observation. Ignore it."

They went through the archway under the lamp into the back courtyard and on through shabby doors into a corridor floored with concrete. Open doors vouchsafed glimpses of piles of nameless waste packed up in plastic bags, others of white tiled kitchens and ranks of aluminium trolleys. They came to a central point where three lifts faced each other across an expanse of worn linoleum. Cobbold pressed all three buttons at once and lights began to flash but it was minutes before any lift appeared.

The next floor was more cheerful. The walls were painted white and the floors were green and white squares of linoleum. As they walked along a corridor Cobbold glanced through a glass door and motioned Charter to look in. A dark-haired young woman in a white coat was sitting huddled over a desk, her shoulders shaking. A young man, also white-coated, was hovering ineffectually, making little dabbing gestures towards her but failing to connect.

Charter walked in. The girl sat up, her eyes anguished, her hair in disarray. It was Ann Prideaux, the young pathologist who had helped Charter on an earlier case by giving her opinion on the medical evidence at a remarkably early stage.

"Good evening, Dr Prideaux," said Charter. "I'm extremely sorry about the death of your colleague."

She gulped and tried to steady herself. "Hello, Mr Charter", she said, and her lip trembled. "It's all so horrible. But I'm glad it's you."

The young man looked at them uncertainly. "I'm Dr Porter," he said. "I didn't know him as well as Ann but we're all devastated. All the girls are in floods. Was it a nutter?"

"That's what it looks like," said Charter. "We'll talk to Dr Prideaux tomorrow when she's feeling better. Come, Sergeant. You too, Dr Porter."

"Me, sir?"

"We'll see you tomorrow too."

"Oh right. Yes of course." He stood to attention. A nervous young man distinctly short of self-confidence. Ann Prideaux, on the other hand, presented a much less timorous appearance in spite of her apparent abandonment to woe.

They went on down the corridor and reached a wide entrance hall where a detective constable was just finishing taking the fingerprints of a short, stocky, bearded man in a jogging suit and anorak who was showing great impatience and annoyance. Catching sight of them he broke away from the policeman and came to meet them, raising one arm in a peremptory gesture. Charter met him halfway across the hall, took the raised hand and shook it firmly.

"Mr Jackson?" he guessed confidently and the hospital administrator looked him in the eye, slight surprise fighting with his air of command.

"That's right. I came over as soon as they brought me the news. Your man on the door didn't realize who I am."

"Detective Chief Superintendent John Charter. They brought you the news, did they, sir? May I ask who brought you the news?"

"My neighbour. Miss Fisher. Our Senior Nursing Officer. She was very distressed. So are we all."

He showed not the slightest sign of distress as he said this.

"Come to my office," he suggested. "I can give you as long as you like tonight. Tomorrow may be a different story."

"Unfortunately," said Charter, "there's a great deal to get through tonight. I fear we shall have to break in on your morning arrangements, Mr Jackson."

Mr Jackson looked a little put out, then he smoothed it over. "Of course. In that case, let my people know when you wish to see me and we'll juggle with the appointments."

"Good night, Mr Jackson."

"Good night, Chief Superintendent."

They walked off to find the mortuary and he stood looking after them, his self-importance slightly wounded.

"He'll probably find he has to make the rounds patting a few people on the head to salve his *amour propre*," said Charter. "Man with a salary like his doesn't easily accept the brush-off even if it's only from the constabulary."

"Might be drying a few tears," suggested the sergeant.

"Ah, yes," said Charter. "Dr Prideaux. Could she be the rejected young woman who was succeeded in Professor Tancred's affections by Fraulein von Treiben? I'm beginning to wonder just how much of a Don Juan this sanctimonious surgeon actually was."

"Sanctimonious, sir?"

"Just guessing, Sergeant."

3

The Pathologist

EXPECTING no surprises from the post-mortem Charter left Detective Inspector Longfield at the mortuary and headed with the sergeant for the station. DCI Cartwright was setting up the Incident Room. They all turned as he came into the room, in some excitement at the arrival of the great man from Penchester whom they usually met only once a year at their interviews.

"I've got a murder squad at the hospital under DI Longfield," said Cartwright. "You'll have seen that we've sealed off the hospital and we're screening all arrivals and fingerprinting all able bodied inmates. I've a team here setting up the search of the files for known weirdos and tramps on this patch. We're on to criminal records and we're circularizing all local stations."

"It may come to house to house from

the mobile control," said Charter, "but I reckon it will be nearer home."

Then he talked to the whole room.

"We're not going to get much joy from the lab on this one at this stage. Open air. Late evening, secluded spot, weapon found at the scene, rough piece of wood — fingerprints fairly dicey. It could have been a straightforward mugging, or an argument between friends or colleagues which turned lethal, possibly by accident. Our first purpose must be to find a shoe to fit the footprint our scene-of-crime friends have been immortalizing in Kaffir D, our second to find the foot that fits the shoe. And then there may be the gear the attacker was wearing to protect himself from the rain. Whatever it was, it must have been bathed in blood from a horrendous head wound. His first preoccupation must have been to destroy it or hide it fast. The shoes too.

"Now we may not have much scope for the lab as yet but as far as motive goes we may be spoilt for choice. Consider the possibilities of grudges against a senior surgeon. Rival colleagues, juniors with their noses out of joint, patients whose operations have gone wrong, their families. And, in medical circles, things are sometimes complicated by Masonic overtones, as some of you may know from your own experience. Always be on the look out for this. In some of the London teaching hospitals almost the entire medical staff are Masons. Then there are built-in difficulties where a hospital is concerned. For instance, how do you comb a hospital for bloodstained clothing when the place is stuffed with legitimate bloodstains which for hygiene's sake must be quickly disposed of? And how do you expect the medical and nursing staff to react to questioning? Well, I'll tell you, and you can take it from me that this is how they will behave. They close ranks. They'll all be on the defensive and they'll be as obstructive as they can possibly be. That's the way the medical profession behave. They call it loyalty. I have another name for it myself. I'm talking to the Press in a few minutes and there'll be announcements on the news from now on. Everyone's going to be shocked at the murder of a top consultant. So let's hope the public start bringing in information right away. The sooner you get those lines manned the better."

A WPC came in with the preliminary PM report. He read it and gathered their attention with a hard look round the room.

"The PM report is straightforward," he said. "He was killed by a blow from the blunt instrument found beside him. It's on its way to the lab but they don't expect much from a rough surface of this kind. There is bruising to the knuckles of the right hand consistent with the delivery of a punch to the jaw or head of, presumably, the murderer. So bruising of the face might be an indication to look out for. On the other hand the victim could have reached up instinctively to fend off the blow and got the bruising that way. He was killed near the spot where he was found and the killer may have tried to drag him away. It looks like unpremeditated on the face of it but always bear in mind that that may be how it's meant to look. One massive blow instantly fatal. The skull fractured and bruising to the brain. Either a man or a very strong woman you might think. But there's a complication. The victim was one of those rare cases where the skull is unusually fragile. So the extent of the damage may bear little relation to the strength of the blow. So — no indication of the strength of the murderer. A fragile little old lady, no. But a reasonably active woman, yes."

Charter then spent some minutes chatting with them all and answering questions, spoke to the waiting members of the Press, went outside for a brief TV interview and finally took Cartwright on one side.

"How about Cobbold? Can you spare him?"

"Anything you say, sir," said Cartwright comfortably. "He's come a long way since that fox-hunting case. Done his Inspector and didn't do at all badly, though it's far too soon in my opinion. But he should get his promotion in a few years' time."

It was long after midnight when Charter headed for home. He was tempted to stop at the White Hart but, having the new house at Rope

Walk, he decided the drive back to Penchester was worth it, and slept in his own bed.

Next morning he looked out at seven o'clock and found that it had rained all night. A strong wind was snaking through the lime trees along the edge of the river, tossing the damp branches. The cloudy sky shaded from pale grey to Chinese white. The river ran in sluggish metallic ripples, lapping quietly but insistently high on the mossy stonework that strengthened the banks.

He decided not to wake Sophie and the children and telephoned later from the station, after checking with the Incident Room and learning nothing of interest. There was no reply from the Mill House (where Sophie still lived) and no good reason for the sudden icy, fearful leap of the heart. They had probably all gone to take Robert to school and then shopping. But he had to force himself not to go straight there to check that Sophie had got home safely. Instead he went to the hospital with the sergeant in search of Mr Harvey Knott, the pathologist, and tracked him down in the surgeons' rest room. Mr Harvey Knott invited them to talk to him then and there.

He was a short man with plentiful greying hair, smooth and glossy with hair cream. He wore a well-tailored suit and well polished hand-made shoes. A quietly authoritative manner matched his appearance.

"There was nothing wrong with him. If this hadn't happened he'd have lived forever. He'd had a little too much to drink but not too much over the odds. He hadn't eaten for several hours. Surgeons tend to forget about meals. No other injuries apart from the dent on the head. You've got it all in the report."

"Did you know him well, sir?"

"Well enough. We dined at each other's houses once or twice a year. Myra Tancred isn't very sociable. So a dinner at home was the only way Gurth ever got her to meet people. He had to get in cooks and washers-up.

"We weren't close colleagues. He was neurosurgery. He was continually being called to the theatre to deal with road accidents, or urgent life-threatening conditions of the brain."

"Do you know anything about his movements last evening?"

"Yes, as a matter of fact I do. Saw him for a moment in here. He'd just swallowed a cup of tea and he was rushing back on to the wards. He told me he'd be busy for another hour and then he was going home."

"What time was that?"

"I should think it must have been about seven o'clock. I went home myself a quarter of an hour later."

"Was he a good surgeon?"

"Extremely good. An excellent Head of Department too."

"It was a good team then. A happy team? They got on well with Professor Tancred?"

"Well of course they did. No reason why they shouldn't."

"Isn't it unusual for a hospital of this size to boast a full blown professor on the staff?"

"Yes. There is a first-class neurosurgical unit at the Penchester Hospital connected with the medical school at the university, Professor Tancred was on the staff of the medical school. He did several operating, and outpatients' sessions over there as well as teaching. We get their students on the wards here and some rather niggardly research funds from time to time."

"So how much time did the professor spend at St Christopher's?"

"He did a couple of outpatients' sessions a week and looked after his patients on the wards."

"So he didn't operate here?"

"No. We haven't the back-up. His patients would be taken to Penchester by ambulance for surgery and they'd come back only after they were out of ITU."

"ITU?"

"Intensive care."

"I see."

"Good neurosurgeons will only operate on high-risk patients where you've got the best nursing and ITU facilities. Lot of smaller hospitals wouldn't have the expert staff you need. They wouldn't be used often enough to maintain their expertise."

"And Professor Tancred was one of the best surgeons?"

"One of the very best."

"Why did he live at St Christopher's?"

"He happened to need a house just at the time this one became vacant and, of course, we were delighted to offer it to him. He'd just been offered the department at Penchester and it gave him a base here. A lot of prestige is attached to having a professor on the staff. He may operate on some of the patients at Penchester not here but they are our patients."

Charter looked consideringly at Mr Harvey Knott and tried a flyer.

"So the professor was a Mason?"

"Oh?"

"Were you aware of it, sir?"

"It's not a thing to chatter about. I can't imagine who told you."

"One tends to look for Masonic connections in professional circles, sir."

"Well, you may as well know. Can't do any harm. We were in the same lodge. And yes we did get on well together. He was a fellow of infinite mirth. I think you might say we all loved him. Didn't see as much of him as I would have liked because of his wife's unsociable behaviour."

"He did have a slight problem with

alcohol didn't he, sir?"

"Nothing to speak of. People tend to drink a little more than they should after lodge meetings. It's only social drinking. He wasn't an alcoholic."

"I imagine his patients must have rather hoped he wouldn't be operating on them the morning after a lodge meeting in that case, sir."

"Nonsense. He was a very fine surgeon. He'd be there on time next morning. You'd never guess he'd been carousing the night before."

"And did this predilection of his affect his relationship with Mrs Tancred?"

Mr Harvey Knott drew his chair a little closer to them, dropped his voice a little and grew confidential.

"It did cause problems in the marriage. Myra Tancred never joined in the social events that draw families together. She resented the time Gurth spent at lodge meetings. There is no doubt they had grown apart."

"And did either of them seek consolation elsewhere?"

Mr Harvey Knott might almost be said to have giggled. "Gurth was rather taken

37

with Silke, the little au pair girl. Perfectly presentable young woman. Good family. Not all that pretty I'd have said but a good little figure. As for Myra, I think she's really well beyond all that. You won't find any secret lovers there. It might have been a relief to poor Gurth if there had been. Mind you one or two people have hinted at a nasty relationship between Myra and the German girl. Women's crushes on each other. That sort of thing. I don't for a moment believe it's more than malicious gossip. The girl doubled as household help and handmaid to Myra's goats. Years ago Myra went overboard on the subject of goats. It used to drive poor old Gurth Tancred out of the house. Goats! I ask you!"

"Beautiful creatures," said Charter. "All sorts of classical overtones to goats."

"Classical poppycock! She spent a fortune of Gurth's hard-earned cash on doing up the outbuildings for them. And the billygoats smell positively rank. She breeds them. Here, in a residential area."

"The milk is excellent for invalids," Charter pointed out. "I expect she makes cheese. Very good, goat cheese. I'd call it a pretty useful enterprise." Then he decided to stop teasing Mr Harvey Knott and got up to go.

Mr Harvey Knott shook hands with them somewhat coldly.

"I have some calls to make," Charter told the sergeant. "I'll go over to the White Hart and meet you at the station in twenty minutes."

He put a call in to Sophie and got the nanny.

"Cathy? Where's Mrs Charter?"

"Oh, Mr Charter, I'm so glad you've phoned," said Cathy. "I tried to get you at the police station. Mrs Charter must have gone off in her car early this morning. When we got up she'd already gone. Then later I got a call from someone she'd asked to give us a message. He said she had a call from one of her clients late last night and it's a film. The photographer had dropped out and they want her to do the stills. They were already on location. She doesn't know how long but it could be a few days. She couldn't let it go because it's a very good director. I was to get Mrs Malvern to help with the children and we're lucky, Mrs Malvern was at home and she's moving in this morning. The only thing is she'll have to go back this evening to see to her cat. She's having kittens and we didn't think she'd be happy in a strange place. Oh and the gentleman who phoned said you have an important case and Mrs Charter said you're not to worry."

Charter put the phone down, puzzled by the solicitude of the final sentence. Sophie never said that sort of thing. It must be a fabrication. Cathy embroidering the story out of kindness. Or else Sophie was up to something and trying to sweeten him into inattention. Again he felt that tiny stab of apprehension. But in the meantime Robert and India would be ecstatic about the visit of their aunt. Clarissa Malvern was Sophie's step-sister. Fifteen years older and a widow. Critical of Sophie on the whole but staunch in time of trouble.

4

The Goats

AFTER a short session in the Incident Room Charter said, "Statements now. Starting with the girl who found the body. Back to the Tancred house. Let's hope they've settled down by now."

They had settled down with a vengeance. Silke wasn't there at all. Myra had sent her off to her English class at the language school in the Market Square. "She has an exam next month," she explained. "I'm not going to let this damage her chances. She'll be back by twelve-thirty."

"I hope you are feeling better," began Charter, and she cut him short sharply.

"I'm perfectly all right," she said. "It was shock. I've had a good night's sleep and I'm sorting things out. No point in being sentimental. Gurth is dead. I shall give the clothes to Oxfam. We'll have

41

to leave this house and the sooner the better."

Charter looked startled by her matter-of-fact manner and she looked at him pityingly.

"Don't look so surprised, Mr Charter," she said. "I have suddenly become a widow in fact, but in essence I've been one for years. First it was the hospital and later the hospital and the girlfriends. And then it was the hospital, the girlfriends and the Masons. I don't suppose anyone told you he was a Mason. It got worse every year. He was very high up at the lodge. I didn't mind giving him up for the patients. But not for the lodge! He was never at home. You know, if you are the wife of an important man like Prof (that's what they call him in the hospital) you don't get asked out without him. They're all afraid of annoying the great man and they won't risk it. It's safer to stay clear. I don't blame them. Their jobs are involved. But it gets lonely. I never went to ladies, nights. It may sound silly but I didn't agree with it so I couldn't pretend I did. And after a time he stopped asking me. I expect he took other women. I never asked. I shan't really miss him much, you know. There isn't anything left to miss. I filled my life with other things."

"Other things?"

"I'll show you. Come along." She took them through the hall into a pantry with a sink and a table laden with flower vases, out into a paved yard with outbuildings round it. On one side was what had originally been a coachhouse. The large double doors were locked and Mrs Tancred took an old-fashioned key out of her pocket and opened them.

"I have to keep them locked up at night," she explained. "They are worth a lot of money. Good morning, my beauties."

More than a dozen long-haired golden goats were moving about in the cool clean interior. The floor was covered with a deep layer of pale gold straw heaped up against the whitewashed walls. The goats turned towards them, lifting up their heads. Some came slowly to their mistress, one by one. Some simply stood and gazed at them coolly and consideringly.

"They are very beautiful," said Charter. "What sort are they?"

"Golden Guernsey."

"Do they live in all year round?" asked the sergeant disapprovingly, and she shook her head. "Of course not. We lead them out to the field beyond the Jacksons for six hours a day all summer. There's a drinking trough out there attached to the mains, and we have a field shelter for them in case it rains. They are delicate creatures."

The coach house was neatly divided. Half of it was made into wooden pens five feet high, so that the goats could peer at each other over the top. At the far end was a raised platform for milking with rings for tethering attached to the wall at collar height. A coiled hose hung on the wall and drainage was cut into the floor in the form of two deep grooves leading to a covered drain. This part of the floor was soaking wet and Myra went to turn off the dripping tap with an impatient exclamation.

"I'll show you the dairy," she said, and took them through a door into a whitewashed room with slatted shelves running round the walls. Two overalls were hanging on the door and beside them two brightly coloured plastic aprons. Along one wall stood large plastic pails covered with white muslin cloths. Two large strainers hung on the wall. At the far end beside the double sink was a tall refrigerator.

"We keep the milk in there," explained Myra, "and they collect it every day. It goes to the hospital and the nursing home."

"Do they ever collect it in the evenings?"

"No. Never. They weren't in the lane last night."

"This must keep you very busy," he said, glancing round.

"Yes. We go out to the woods to gather willow branches for them. Silke loves that. We groom them and we milk them and we strain the milk and put it in the cans to be collected."

As they walked back she stretched out her hands to caress the nearest of the goats, stroking the silky flanks and taking the slender heads in her hands. "There, Indigo, come, Tendril, come, my sweet Periwinkle," she crooned, the ancient goddess smile on her lips again, the same look she had turned on Silke the night before.

"So," said Charter gently, "you filled your life with the goats and then Silke came."

"Yes," she said. "Having Silke to help me makes it all so much pleasanter. We work together. We talked till late last night and we're going to buy a hill farm in Wales. Sheep and goats."

"Will Silke's parents agree to that?" asked Charter.

"Why not? They sent her over here to learn English. I'll teach her about poetry and Shakespeare. She'll be happy."

She put the goats aside and led the way back into the house.

"Mrs Tancred," said Charter, "where will you get the money for the farm in Wales? This house belongs to the hospital."

"Yes it does. But we kept our old house in Hampshire. And there must be investments. I'll have to see the lawyer. For the first time in years I feel as if there may be something to look forward to."

Charter shook his head at this and got up.

"We'll want a statement from you, Mrs Tancred, about your movements last night. Purely routine. Anything you can think of which might have a bearing on your husband's death."

She frowned. "Yes," she said, "I'll do anything I can to help you. I didn't want him to die like that but don't try to make me be sad. I can't let myself get into a state. Don't try to make me." Her voice rose on this and he said soothingly, "I understand. Now, Mrs Tancred, when Frauline von Treiben comes home I'll want to see her. Perhaps, as you are *in loco parentis*, you will want to be present."

He turned away and she looked at him angrily and leaned forward to seize him by the wrist.

He looked at her with his eyebrows raised and she let go of him.

"I'm sorry," she said. "But I know you were telling me my duty when you said that about in *loco parentis*. But you must understand. You talk as if we corrupted her. It was Silke who went after Gurth.

47

And at first he was just too vain to resist her. May I start packing things up now? Your men have been here and they've taken things away. Our clothes and shoes. Have they finished?"

"Yes. That's all right, Mrs Tancred. But, of course, we'll leave a man on the front door for your protection."

"Thank you," she said tartly with an ironical look that showed she was aware that that sort of protection worked both ways.

5

Silke von Treiben

CHARTER hurried across the Market Square to the White Hart and dialled Sophie's number.

"Clarissa!" he said. "You're so good to come. How are the children?"

"Robert's at school but India's here baking a cake."

"Give her a hug from me. But, Clarissa, where is Sophie? I've got to talk to her."

She sounded worried. "I don't know, John. It must be off in the wilds or she'd come back to be with the children at night."

"Why didn't she phone herself? Who rang for her?"

"I don't know, John. I wasn't here. But I'll ask Cathy. She's gone out shopping."

"Clarissa, what's she up to?"

"I honestly don't know any more than you do, John, but I'm damned sure

49

she's up to something. It's not like her to leave the children. It must be something serious. Can you come round and talk?"

"I promise you I'll be there the minute I can get away. Just now, of all times, I'm doing a murder."

"Oh Lord! Well, come as soon as you can."

"She's sure to telephone to know how the children are. Tell her to phone me whatever time of the day or night."

"I'll tell her. Don't worry, John. She's pretty sensible on the whole. Most of the time."

"It's the rest of the time I'm worried about."

"Poor John! You should have married a more solid and sensible spouse."

"If she's not careful, I will," he said bitterly, and Clarissa laughed.

"No, you won't," she said. "It's a shameful waste. I won't try to ring you unless she phones. You ring here."

"Right. Thanks, Clarissa."

He went back to the Tancred house his whole body tense and the tight feeling in his chest that he always got when he knew there were disasters looming ahead. This was no way to start a murder inquiry.

At the Tancred house he found Myra, Silke and the sergeant drinking coffee in the kitchen.

"Right," he said. "May we interview Frauline von Treiben here?"

Myra made a gesture of assent and went out of the room. The sergeant cleared away the coffee cups and took out his memo pad.

Charter began. "Frauline von Treiben," he said, "I would like you to understand quite clearly that this is a purely routine interview. In a murder inquiry it is incumbent on us to talk to everyone connected in any way with the victim, and with the person who found the body. This doesn't mean that we suspect anyone of anything as yet."

"I understand," she said. "I am not a fool."

"Then can you tell me what you were doing in the lane last night?"

She looked at him broodingly under thick dark eyebrows. From the nose up she was lovely but a heavy mouth and jaw made the face look more commonplace than it seemed at first sight.

"Call me Silke," she said. "I'm only a student. You don't have to be so stuffy."

"Very well. Now answer the question."

"I went to a concert at the institute," she said. "It ended at eight-forty. I heard the clock strike nine as I walked across the Square."

"Could you give me some details of the concert, Miss?" asked the sergeant.

"Bach Brandenberg Concertos."

"And when you saw the body," went on Charter, "you recognized it at once?"

"I saw the shoes. He wears them to play squash and he often keeps them on because his feet hurt him in the leather ones."

"And you didn't see anyone near the body?"

"No, not really. There was something moving over there but it was raining. The light was bad."

"And when you saw him you knew at once that he was dead?"

"I thought he had fallen and I bent over him and then I saw the blood and the hole in the head. It was frightful."

"You were very distressed?"

"I screamed like a fool. I never screamed so in my life before. And then the police came and took me home."

"And you identified the body for them?"

"I told them it was the professor from the house where I am staying. It was a shock to poor Myra. I came with the police and my hands were shaking like a jellyfish. I could not stop them. And she made me drinks and put me by the fire. She is very brave."

"Were you happy in this house?"

"Quite happy."

"And did you like the professor?"

"Yes, I liked him very much."

"What sort of man was he?"

"Like other men. He did what he wanted."

"Can you imagine why anyone would take a heavy piece of wood and hit him over the head?"

"I don't know why. They must have hated him very much."

"You don't know of anyone who might have wanted to injure him?"

"Myra told you he made love to me and then he stopped making love to me. But I wouldn't kill him for that. It doesn't trouble me if a man loves me and then he doesn't love me anymore. There are plenty of men. Perhaps that other woman in the hospital killed him. The one he loved before me."

"What would your parents think about all this? Won't they want you to go home?"

"I don't know. They have other things to think about. In any case he isn't here anymore. Myra says she will look after me."

"Would you like that?"

"It's OK by me. I love to be with animals. I love the country. She says Wales is very beautiful. I don't like to be in Hamburg in the flat. I like to be more free."

"I see."

Charter was somewhat nonplussed. Afterwards as they sat in the snug at the White Hart with beer and sandwiches, he said to the sergeant, "Those women seem to think it doesn't matter what they say to us. Is it innocence or is it double bluff? They must know they're suspects. They both have motives for murder."

"Do you think, sir, that Mrs Tancred could be playing a deep game? She gave us the motive for Silke. Perhaps she *was* jealous of the affair and the hints of her own relationship with the girl could be so much camouflage."

"Yes. Mrs Tancred could have waited for her husband in the lane, hit him over the head and gone back home, leaving him for Silke to find. She knew Silke would be coming that way soon."

"Now, we'd better get on to the hospital administrator. What do you bet, Derek, that he's a Mason too? He has the air."

"No bets, sir. He is. Didn't you notice?" And he made a sign.

"Is that so? Where are my wits?"

6

The Hospital Administrator

MR JACKSON was not as affable as he had been the night before and he was making no secret signs. Charter made a mental note that Mr Harvey Knott had made a quick phone call and put the hospital administrator on his guard. This, or something else, had made him distinctly ill at ease and he fiddled nervously with a pen, a blotter and the strap of his gold Rolex watch.

"Please sit down Mr Charter. Will you have coffee? Anything else? Right. How are you getting on?"

"Slowly, sir."

"I hope we'll get some answers soon. It's unsettling for the staff. They tell me the nurses say they won't go out at night until you've found him. And it can't be doing the reputation of St Christopher's any good."

"It hasn't done Professor Tancred any good either, sir, and that's where my duty lies. St Christopher's must take its chance. Can you give me an account of your movements last night?"

Mr Jackson looked deeply offended. "Do you really think this is necessary?" he asked.

"I'm afraid so."

The sergeant took up his memo pad.

"Just routine, sir," he said reassuringly.

"I was in my office all afternoon and at six o'clock I walked home. I'm usually here until seven or eight o'clock, but it was my wife's birthday and we were having a celebration dinner. Just the two of us."

"And you saw nothing unusual in the lane? No one hanging about?"

"I'd have sent for the hospital security people if I had."

"I imagine the professor will be a great loss to St Christopher's?"

"Yes. The neurological unit at Penchester will be missing their star member of staff."

"And won't he be missed equally here?"

"It's not quite the same. He brought us patients but he didn't actually operate here so most of the credit went to Penchester."

"But he was an important member of the staff?"

"Oh yes. I think you could say he was the big shot around here. He had an international reputation. Spent some time every year travelling to medical conferences."

"Wasn't that bad for your budget?"

"Not at all. In fact it helped us out. Gurth Tancred was one of those consultants who do what they want to do without consulting the plans made by the administration. We have plans for each period ahead. Otherwise we couldn't budget. There's a lot more to pay for in hospital than top surgeons and their patients. We've got the boilers to keep going and the staff to pay and all the negotiating that that entails. Some consultants overshoot the mark by massive amounts. Gurth Tancred was one of those. 'Creeping incrementalism' we call it. Exceeding the plan and leaving us to find how to pay for it."

"He must have been a bit of a headache for you."

"He was a pain in the neck. Our Senior Nursing Officer discovered that on one occasion he had exceeded her nursing budget by thousands of pounds simply by forgetting to charge his private patients for nursing care. He simply charged them for the hotel and medical charges. We had to sort it out."

"And did you?"

"Oh yes. But the fact that he spends some of his time abroad helps as he can't operate while he's away, so that immediately cuts the number of operations he does."

"Are you aware of any circumstances which might have contributed to Professor Tancred's murder?"

"No. Of course I'm not. He was an outstandingly able surgeon and a very pleasant man. Tremendously popular in the hospital and with the patients and their families."

"I see. Did Professor Tancred belong to the same lodge as you? I believe he was in the same one as Mr Harvey Knott. The Penchester lodge I imagine."

A look of great annoyance came over Mr Jackson's face and for a moment Charter thought he wasn't going to answer but he said at last, "Yes, he did."

"Was he the highest of the hospital contingent in that lodge?"

"Yes. As it happens, he was."

"So he was a good Mason?"

"Of course he was."

"Influential?"

"Naturally, in the position he held."

"And there was no unpleasantness between him and the Masons?"

"Quite the contrary. The Masons looked after him and protected him. I assure you no Mason could possibly be involved in this dreadful business. It has nothing to do with the Masons and I rather object to this line of questioning."

"The Masons protected him? Why should he need the protection of the Masons?"

Mr Jackson was sweating visibly. "I didn't mean that he needed any specific form of protection. I was trying to explain that the Masons tend to protect their brethren if they can, not to make trouble for them. Just a general observation."

"I see." Charter looked at him hard. "So you and Mr Harvey Knott and Professor Tancred would support each other if any controversial matter arose in the hospital."

"No. That isn't at all what I meant to imply. We would be completely impartial in the hospital. But, of course, knowing each other well, meeting often at the lodge and the ladies' nights does help with human relationships. We could smooth differences over with the welfare of the hospital and the patients in mind."

"I see. And you know of no incidents in the hospital which might have a bearing on the death of your professor?"

"Discreditable incidents do you mean? Who ordered you to take up this line of questioning? There was nothing of the kind."

"I have heard rumours that the professor may have gone in for indiscreet behaviour with some of the female staff."

Mr Jackson mopped his brow and seemed to cool down. "I don't think

61

he had any actual affairs in the hospital but many of the women seemed to have fallen for him. He was a very good-looking man. Rather rumpled but women seem to like that. None of this will be made public will it? We have to be careful with the press. They are only too ready to give us bad publicity."

"I hope not. Do you know any names of women involved with the Professor?"

"Well, it's only rumour. One hesitates to repeat gossip. But Dr Prideaux might be able to help you. She is in the hospital today. Would you like to see her now?" He stood up hopefully, but Charter remained seated, regarding Jackson with an unnerving gaze.

"It was a tramp," said Mr Jackson feebly. "Must have been. No one in this hospital. No one."

Charter stood up. "We'll see Professor Tancred's team now. Names please, Mr Jackson."

7

The Registrar

WILLIAM PARCHMENT, the senior surgical registrar, was a curly-haired young man of athletic build. He was sitting behind a desk in his white coat, making entries in a patient's file. He looked up at them and blinked. He was very pale and the shadows under his eyes were almost black.

"Good morning, Dr Parchment," said Charter, then, in concern, "Are you all right, sir?"

Parchment had rubbed a hand over his eyes and was yawning horribly.

"Oh, hello," he said. "Yes, I'm all right. They told us you'd want to see us all as soon as possible. Could we get on with it pretty smartly? If you don't mind. I've been on call for more than fifty hours and I may be operating again tonight. We've had two nasty accidents in twenty-four hours and if I don't crash out soon I'll be out on my feet."

"Right, sir. We'll be as brief as possible. Have you any idea who might have wanted to kill Professor Tancred?"

"No. No idea. I don't even know what happened. How was he killed? I've literally either been in theatre or crashed out on a couch for the last forty-eight hours."

"He was beaten over the head with a blunt instrument."

"Oh God!" His hands trembled on the desk and he snatched them off it and put them in his lap.

"Was it a psychopath?" he asked.

"We can't say yet. It may have been. All the possibilities are being exhaustively checked, but it takes time. I hear he was a good surgeon."

"On his day he was brilliant."

"Does that mean he had off days?"

"Everyone has."

"Would not being on his day have anything to do with his evenings at the lodge?"

"The lodge?"

"I take it you are not a Freemason yourself?"

64

"I should bloody well think not. You mean to tell me Prof was a Mason?"

Charter felt the astonishment was somewhat theatrical.

"Along," he said, "with Mr Jackson and Mr Harvey Knott. I wonder whether perhaps Professor Tancred was sometimes late in the theatre on the mornings after lodge meetings and whether he might, in those circumstances, have been a little worse for wear. And whether perhaps his Masonic brethren among the surgeons (I feel sure there were some), might have protected him from the consequences by, perhaps, taking over part of his list."

"Prof would never have let anyone take over any part of his list unless he was completely *hors de combat*."

"Were there rivalries among the consultants?"

"Of course."

"Anything serious enough to have led to murder?"

"I've no idea. I'm far too busy opening people up and closing them up, trying to patch them up, putting the pieces together and trying to make them work."

"Should Professor Tancred have

delegated more operations to junior staff than he did?"

William Parchment looked up at him and smiled. "I see," he said. "You've worked out a scenario in which the ambitious young registrar feels he is being kept back because his superior hogs all the best ops? That's a non-starter. Prof was absolutely correct. He gave us what we could do. No more. No less. He was a brilliant guy to work for. We were all his protégés."

"He must have been a good man."

"The best bloke in the world."

"Do you know anything about Professor Tancred's exploits with women in the hospital?"

A deep flush rose from the young man's neck, flooded his face, clashing with the tight ginger curls and faded, leaving him whiter than before.

"I see you do."

"He didn't go in for exploits. He simply fell in love with them. He had a short fling with Dr Prideaux. Lasted only a few weeks and then she saw the light. He wasn't exactly devoted to his wife but he wasn't the sort of bloke who would

66

ever have deserted anyone. Dr Prideaux soon realized that there was no future in it and gave him the push."

"She gave him the push?"

"Oh yes. He was far too old for her."

"So Dr Prideaux didn't bear a grudge against him?"

"Of course not."

"And you don't bear a grudge on her behalf?"

"Come on, sir, this is the twentieth century. Ann's not an infant in arms. She knew what she was doing. It was an aberration on her part."

"You're a lucky man. I have a high respect for her."

"Oh, it was you, wasn't it? She stuck her neck out for you on that dead master of foxhounds business? I told her she was a fool at the time but it worked out all right in the end."

"I was very grateful to her. Now, as a matter of routine, we have to ask you for an account of your movements last evening. Where were you?"

"I was either in theatre operating or in the sports centre catnapping."

"Were you in the theatre between nine and ten-thirty?"

"No. I was cat-napping then. I can't sleep in the evenings up there where all the action is. There's too much noise. So I go down to the sports centre. It's quiet down there and they have couches for aromatherapy. I've got the bleep so it doesn't matter where I am as long as I'm on the premises. After eleven it quietens down so I go back upstairs."

"Can anyone substantiate that?"

"I expect old Lily can."

"Lily?"

"The cleaning woman. I can only go there when Lily's about. Otherwise it's locked up. I go down when I'm really pooped. Lily's a right old dear. She brings me tea to wake me up when she's ready to go."

The sergeant made a note. "Interview Lily, sports centre."

"There's just one thing more," said Charter. "I believe that Professor Tancred operated at Penchester. How much time do you spend over there with him?"

"It varies. Sometimes when he has a heavy list I'll be over there two days a week. Then I do my own minor procedures here. I do my stint at casualty over there when they're under pressure. I'm forever underway between Penchester and Stumpington."

"It sounds as if you'd do better to amalgamate the two hospitals."

"We may do that. There are all sorts of plans in the air. Prof wasn't at all keen on any of them. He liked things to stay as they were."

"Would he have the clout to see that they did?"

"Well, he was the kingpin at Penchester. He was the neurosurgical unit there. But no one's irreplaceable as we are now going to find out. Unfortunately. May I get on now?"

"Thank you, sir. That will do for the present."

They went down to the front hall.

8

Oscar Hay, MP

CHARTER now sent Cobbald to the station, left the hospital, and went to the White Hart. He got his car out of the car park and headed for the Mill House, five miles upriver from Penchester and ten miles out of Stumpington, where Sophie still lived with the children. There he found Cathy washing-up and Clarissa reading a story to Robert. India was already in bed.

Robert came bounding over to jump up at him. Cathy took one look at his face and came to take Robert's hand and lead him off upstairs.

Clarissa poured them both Scotch and water and they sat at the kitchen table to confront the problem.

"Still no word?"

"None at all."

"No ideas?"

"None, John. It doesn't make sense.

70

Why not tell us at least the location
and the name of the director? Surely she
would phone, however busy they are on
the set."

"You think there is no film?"

"I don't know what to think."

"She may still phone tonight. I suppose
the first day would be pretty hectic. It's
only this morning we got the message
after all. She'll phone tomorrow."

"I'm sure she will."

"Well, let me know the minute she
does. Can you really stay, Clarissa?"

"I would even if I couldn't, but I
can."

He kissed her cheek and got up to
go.

"What would we do without you?
Thank you, dear Clarissa. I'll be back
tomorrow and if there's no word I
promise you I'll set things in motion.
We'll know where she is by tomorrow
evening."

Then he went home to Penchester for
a breather, a steak and salad and a half
bottle of Rioja.

It was at 8.30 that the phone rang.
He switched off the record player and

reached for the phone.

"Charter," he said.

It wasn't Sophie. A deep, pleasant, male voice which sounded familiar.

"Detective Chief Superintendent John Charter?"

"Yes."

"This is Oscar Hay."

"How do you do, sir." He threw off his fatigue and forced himself to concentrate.

"I believe you are in charge of the investigation into the death of Gurth Tancred?"

"That is so, sir."

"I have information which may be relevant to your inquiries. It is very sensitive material. I have a request to make which you may not be able to go along with. I ask you simply to hear me out and then, when you've heard what I've got to say, to give me your answer."

"Go ahead, sir."

"I would like to meet you this evening down there in Penfoldshire. Wherever you wish. The meeting is to be completely unofficial and off the record. When we've

72

talked and you've heard what I have to tell you, you can decide what's to be done about it and I will do exactly as you advise."

"If the object is privacy I suggest you come here to my house. But I have to tell you, that it is most unlikely that I could keep such a meeting secret."

"I know that. I should be there before ten. Rather late but we're both accustomed to keeping late hours. The address?"

"Number four, Rope Walk, Penchester."

"Presumably near the river."

"On the edge of it. East of the Cathedral precinct."

"Good. I'll be there."

Charter walked over to the painted chest and poured himself a strong whisky. Fetching *Who's Who* from the bookshelf, he sat on the bentwood rocking chair and looked up Oscar Hay. HAY. Oscar Hetherington, son of the late General Hetherington Hay, was married to Mary Hardingly, daughter of the Dean of Penchester, had two sons and one daughter, deceased, was educated at Winchester and New College, had gained second class Honours in Politics, Philosophy and Economics, was a director of Railton and Rourke, the publishers, and belonged to the Carlton Club and the MCC.

Charter had seen Oscar Hay on television in political discussions and in the Commons. He was short, strongly built, fair-haired, handsome, and exuded forcefulness. When attacked he was capable of conveying raw menace. You could see that the interviewers detested him. They looked at him coldly and narrowly and never laughed at his jokes. How could Sophie possibly . . . ? He pulled himself together and went back to Oscar Hay.

He must think now as he had never thought before.

What had happened to Sophie? What more likely than that when she marched out of the house, having heard him promise to join his colleagues in twenty minutes, she would assume he was too busy to help her and would drive off to Stumpington to call on Professor Tancred and ask him for the letter. Could Sophie have come upon the murderer somewhere in Stumpington that night?

She would have had no idea that the incident he had promised to go to on the telephone was a murder. When she got to the hospital the police were already on the scene. Was it possible she might have seen the murderer somewhere there — perhaps seen someone where he didn't want to be seen? Could she have noticed, perhaps, a bloodstain, or some terrible distress not adequately hidden? And could the murderer have thought that later on her evidence in court might tell conclusively against him?

His heart sank. He went to the chest and poured himself another large whisky. And this time it was he who, contrary to his usual practice, tossed half of it off at once. He was very tired and he shut his eyes for a moment. At once in his mind's eye he saw an imaginary screen and written across it in large black letters, the words he had refused even to consider —

Sophie is dead.

He winced and opened his eyes. But she wasn't. Of course she wasn't. She was busy on a film set, part of a team, happily furthering her career. She knew the children would be safe and happy with Clarissa there. She knew Clarissa would drop everything and come. Sophie would come home tomorrow wondering what all the fuss was about. But if this were true why didn't she phone?

Suppose it was Oscar Hay who had done murder and mustn't be known to have been in Stumpington that night then a chance encounter with Sophie in Stumpington would mean stark danger for him. He would react by wanting to stop her. To stop her for ever. But would he dare to do it? If he had already killed Tancred, then, yes. What's a second murder if you think you've already got away with the first?

Could the man have killed or kidnapped Sophie and then phoned a bogus message to explain that she was working on a film? Sophie certainly might pose a threat to him. There were earlier incidents where sexual peccadilloes had lost men their place. Sophie had said Hay didn't know she had lost the letter but was it not possible that Professor Tancred might have told him where the letter was and threatened to use it against him? That would put Hay right there among the suspects. Tomorrow he must be asked to make a statement.

And then he dwelt on another possibility that might occur to his colleagues when they heard the story of the letter. Could Sophie herself have bludgeoned Professor Tancred to death? Physically there was no doubt that she could. Sophie was very strong. She had been carrying heavy cameras and lighting equipment about for years.

But if Sophie had done the murder she had come straight to Rope Walk from the scene of the crime and all the talk about the letter and asking Charter to retrieve it for her had been sheer hypocrisy. That wasn't Sophie. There was no need for her to mention the letter at all. And knowing how well he knew her this would be the last place she would come to. She would know he'd see through her. So the answer to the question was he embarking on a murder inquiry into a murder done by his ex-wife was, no. But she was a vital witness and tomorrow he must set the Force on to finding her unless she telephoned or Hay had news of her. Did that mean he'd got to come off the inquiry? If they said so he'd resign from the Force and carry on alone. No one was going to get there as fast as he was. He'd see the ACC tomorrow and tell him about Hay and put the whole thing to him.

Having formulated these thoughts, he washed out his mouth to avoid welcoming Oscar Hay with whisky fumes on his breath, turned the record player on again and went back to Monteverdi. At a quarter to ten he fixed up the recording device and then he was ready.

The doorbell rang.

Charter opened the door and stepped back sharply. A broad figure was standing on the top step, very close to the door so that he could shelter from the rain under the small projecting porch. In the lamplight and the rain and the mist that was streaming up from the river Oscar Hay loomed in the doorway. Then he came in smiling and taking off his raincoat. His wet hair and eyebrows looked pale and almost phosphorescent in the lamplight and Charter saw that he was not blond but prematurely grey.

Then Hay took him by the arm. "Look!" he said. "Snap!" and he turned back to the door and pointed to the two racing green MGs parked in the street.

"That must be yours, is it? The 2.01? And mine's the Turbo. Your guv'nors wouldn't much like it, would they, if you drove one of those? Bad luck."

"I'm afraid, sir," said Charter, "that they wouldn't much like it that you do."

Oscar Hay's thick pale lips parted in a smile. The light-blue eyes remained cold. "Then," he said, "it's just as well that in England a politician outranks a policeman."

Charter took the coat and hung it up. He turned no answering smile on his visitor. The look of the man was so unpleasant to him that it made his flesh creep. He wouldn't have him sitting in the easy chairs where he was accustomed to sit with his friends. They would face each other across the deal table near the Aga.

Hay never took his eyes off Charter. He took the back of the upright chair in his hand and sat down without looking at it. Charter felt the expressionless eyes were locked on his in an attempt to exert a sort of hypnotic force. He stared back, striving to command the revulsion he felt and at the same time resisting the blatant attempt at domination.

He shook his head to throw off the hypnotic effect, banished the thought of Sophie going to bed with this man lest he should be tempted to punch him on the nose, and concentrated on the man himself, the man here at this moment, with a purpose or plan which Charter must unravel and stitch up again to suit his own purposes. It was quite possible that it was only his own idiosyncratic reaction to the man that made him quite certain that he was dealing with a predator. Sophie's lover, the man whose reputation Sophie had asked him to protect. Well, to hell with that. This was a new scenario. And then, to his dismay, he saw once again in his head that imaginary screen with the words across it standing out in black — *Sophie is dead*.

They sat down.

He said, "This isn't a social call and you are driving so nothing to drink."

"Much better not."

"So what can I do for you, Mr Hay?"

"It concerns your sister, Mr Charter."

"My sister?"

"Sophie."

"Ah," he said, "that sister," and he crushed down a sudden smile at Sophie's cunning and the reason for that cunning. She had tried, Sophie had actually tried, to protect him, Charter, from scandal.

"She told me her name was Sophie Saltram, but I knew her real name is Charter. I asked if she was related to you when she told me she lived near Penchester. I've had a house at Fillingham for quite a while as you probably know. You've got to have a house in the constituency. So I knew who you were. I followed that inquiry into the death of that dreadful fellow, Charles Hardcastle. How on earth he got to be MFH I can't imagine. Fellow who didn't know who his own grandfather was."

"As he didn't take his grandfather out hunting with him I don't think that was particularly relevant to his capacity as MFH," said Charter.

"Well, quite apart from all that the fellow was a perfect shit. Never mind. Sophie didn't want to admit that you were related but she gave in when she saw I'd already hoisted it in. She explained how she went back to her maiden name after her marriage broke up. She says she tends to ask your advice about everything. That's why I decided I'd bring this to you. As her brother you'd have her interests at heart."

"So?"

"Two days ago I had a call from Gurth Tancred. He told me he had come into possession of a letter I had written to your sister. It was a letter the tenor of which was unmistakable. He said he would give it back to me if I promised to leave Sophie alone."

"And if not?"

"He'd send it to the Prime Minister."

"Just the letter? Surely that wouldn't accomplish much?"

"Well, it's not just the question of a prospective minister's morals. I said some rather offensive things about the Prime Minister to amuse Sophie."

"I see."

"I told Tancred that I didn't intend to see Sophie again. That sort of thing isn't really on for a cabinet minister. So he suggested I should come down to meet him and he would then give me the letter. Before that could happen I heard he had been murdered."

"So where is the letter now?"

"I imagine it must be somewhere among his things. Either at his home or at the hospital. God knows where. He was inefficient, muddled and careless."

"Then you already knew Professor Tancred before the incident?"

"Yes, I've known him for three or four years. We spend our summers down here as well as most weekends. A year ago he treated my daughter when she developed a tumour. My daughter died. In circumstances like that you get to know the surgeon."

"I'm very sorry to hear that."

"Thank you."

"So what can I do for you?"

"If the tabloids got hold of that letter

it would do me harm. I want to know, will it be necessary to make it public?"

"Not necessarily. It depends on whether it's found to throw any light on the circumstances of Professor Tancred's death."

"Of course I can't ask you outright to suppress it."

"No."

"But it would be very unpleasant for your sister if it did come out."

"Yes, it would."

"Then you can't do anything?"

"No."

"Then I've had a journey for nothing. God damn the little bitch! Where is she anyway? I've been trying to get hold of her all day long."

Charter looked at him stonily.

Oscar Hay stood up, swung on his heel and marched out of the room and out of the house, shutting the front door after him with a snap. A few moments later the MG Turbo roared into life and away into the night. Charter willed the traffic cops to gather vigilantly on the road to London.

He poured himself a small whisky,

faced the fact that everything must be revealed to the ACC as soon as possible and went to bed half convinced that within a few hours he might be out of a job.

9

Sophie's Folder

IN the morning he rang Godfrey
Baldwin's secretary and made an
appointment to see him. The ACC
was in London all day so he arranged
to breakfast with him at his house the
next day.

Charter checked with the Incident
Room and found no leads had come in
from the public, nothing interesting had
emerged from the records and there had
been no finds of bloodstained clothing or
shoes to fit the imprint on the lane.

It now occurred to him that the next
thing to do was to search Mill House
for clues among Sophie's papers about
her whereabouts.

The sun was shining behind a thin
haze that softened the stark outlines
of the bare trees. A light steam was
rising from the stubble fields and blowing
away into the mist. The gentle slopes of

Penfold Chase receded into the distance, some of the hills as pale as water, others dark and clearly outlined with here a clump of trees sharply defined and drawn as if with a fine nib and Indian ink, and there another, opaque and indistinct.

Cathy came to the door.

"Oh, hello, Mr Charter!" she said. "Did you want to see the children?"

"Not if I can help it. Not today, Cathy. I've got to look through some papers. It won't take long."

He went upstairs and into the room he and Sophie had shared for six years. She still slept in the four-poster bed they'd bought in Oxford. The dressing-room beyond was now used for her photographic equipment, files and a small fridge for film. It took him half an hour to go through her papers and it was right at the back of the wardrobe that he found a folder labelled *St C's and OH*.

Inside the folder he found a collection of photographs of the staff of St Christopher's. There was one labelled Miss Fisher, the Senior Nursing Officer. There she was again, talking earnestly with a ward sister. Dr Parchment was there kitted out in surgical gear, boots and cap and rubber gloves. There was Myra Tancred looking almost beautiful, smiling her goddess smile among her goats. There was an old lady in an overall with curl papers in her wispy grey hair, grinning wickedly into the lens. Next was a picture of Mr Jackson, minatory at his desk. Then Mr Harvey Knott, supreme among his instruments in the mortuary.

The biggest collection was of a man of medium height, broad shouldered, silver hair cropped so that the satisfactory bone structure of head and face appeared to advantage. It was a profoundly kindly face. There was an ingenuousness there, a sort of confident smiling innocence, that must have been hard to capture on film. He'd looked quite different on the mortuary slab.

He began to read the accompanying sheets of foolscap. On the first page was a short piece headed *Tit for Tat, for Gurth*. It seemed to be notes for the opening paragraphs of an article on Oscar Hay which could not be described as admiring.

Brilliant young cabinet minister-to-be or sinister slimy self server? At Westminster it's difficult, so they say, to tell.

Anyone can see that the interviewers on TV don't like him. That may be because it's well known that he once set out to tear a young interviewer to pieces on the screen and succeeded so well that the young man hasn't been heard of since. He looks as if he's ready to go for the jugular at the slightest provocation. But on the other hand the women in his life say he can be funny and kind and self-deprecating and takes a lot of flak with equanimity. Some people adore him but they are on the whole those who don't work for him.

He admits he is unpopular in some quarters and claims that anyone who accomplishes anything useful is bound to make enemies on the way up. And on the way up he most certainly is. The word at Westminster is that the PM is waiting only for an auspicious moment to bring him into the Cabinet. He is known to be one of the courtiers. Those

*who can make the Prime Minister laugh
and who stand by with the cloak to
throw on the ground before her feet.*

That was all.

Neatly docketed beside this sheet were
photographs of Oscar Hay. Sophie had
produced pictures which were focused
solely on Hay without anything to distract
from the central figure. Squat, powerful,
menacing.

The last envelope contained a snapshot
of a thin and pale little girl of about
eight years of age sitting cross-legged in
a smocked linen nightdress on a hospital
bed gazing into the lens with a faint
smile on her lips. Charter turned over
the print. Pencilled in on the back was
the name Caroline with a large question
mark. Under this Sophie had written.
'*This* is why? Caroline Hay?'

Cathy came to the door. "Clarissa's
just off on the school run and I'd like
to take India and go with her. We've got
shopping to do. Is that all right?"

"That's fine, Cathy." he said. "I'm just
off myself. I'll take these papers with me.
If Mrs Charter should happen to come

back will you tell her that I'll be bringing them back as soon as possible?"

"Of course."

"I'm very grateful to you, Cathy, Is everything all right? You and Clarissa getting on?"

"Oh yes, of course we are. She's lovely. The children adore her and she's very kind to me."

"I'm glad. That's a relief. Off you go."

He drove to Stumpington and ordered coffee at the White Hart. There he read the rest of the papers in Sophie's folder.

They were headed *Notes for a TV treatment.*

An old-fashioned building in a country town. Georgian facade. Courtyards and tree-lined lanes and a few acres of grounds with the odd modern prefabricated building and a brace of picturesque staff cottages.

Professor Tancred is not your pompous consultant. You can say what you like to him. If you go too far he will laugh at you and tell you you are talking nonsense. He plays squash regularly and swims every day in the hospital sports complex.

I talked to Lily, the old lady who keeps the sports centre clean.

"What do you think of Professor Tancred?" I asked her.

"I bleeding well worship him," she said. "That's what! If one of your loved ones is poorly, you go to the Prof, dear."

Miss Jackie Fisher, the Senior Nursing Officer, who lives in a similar Georgian house to the Professor, tells me that his team do often burst into applause at some extraordinary surgical feat. Dr Porter, a young surgical registrar who works in the professor's team and has been trained by him. "He's a tremendous bloke," said Dr Porter.

The neat typing stopped here and Sophie had scribbled over the rest of the page in her large round hand:

That's all he wants to say. They're all the same. Nervous. Stubborn. All I ever get from any of them is bland

92

praise of Prof. Has someone got to them? Have they been told to clam up or is it an instinct they were born with? Are they paranoid or am I such a hopeless interviewer that I've frightened them all off? Is there a scandal? Has he killed a patient? Is he a drunk? And why is Oscar doing it? He's a complete pig. I know he is. And Gurth's a love but a bit of a soak? I hope, I hope, I hope it isn't that. I must stop. Tell Oscar. No go.

Then further down the page she'd written in large letters: *STOP STOP STOP*.

Charter took up the photograph of the child again.

This is why? . . . Why, what? Why Oscar Hay has asked her, or commissioned her, to take these pictures? To help him get together the research for a television programme that would finish Gurth Tancred as a surgeon. That must be it. And Sophie doesn't much like it when she realizes what Hay is up to. That's why she writes the beginning of the critical article on him — the *Tit for*

Tat, for Gurth. And then she loses the letter to Tancred and he wants to use it, not because he disapproves of Hay's morals, but because he wants to stop Hay from attacking him. For what? Medical malpractice?

The last envelope in the folder produced a bundle of letters. He drew them out and looked at them with distaste. He frowned and thought hard and then he opened them. He had to find Sophie and all rules must go by the board. Reluctantly he began to read and soon he was transfixed.

It was difficult to believe that the Oscar Hay he had met could have written those letters. They were gentle and funny and thoughtful and loving. Then, with a shock, he saw a familiar line which, addressed to Sophie, was a stroke of genius —

She gave, she took, she wounded, she appeased.

He was suddenly furious to think that that coarse man could have quoted to Sophie lines from Raleigh, one of his own favourite poets. And then he thought, I never quoted poetry to her, and felt a deep sense of sadness and waste and guilt as if he were to blame for everything that had gone wrong between them. And he remembered another line from the same despairing poem which could as well be addressed by himself to Sophie as by the Ocean to Scinthia: *She is gone, she is lost, she is found, she is ever fair.*

He folded the letters and put them back into the folder. They wouldn't help him to find her.

He must work out where all this new information could lead them and wished that it was hard evidence.

Sophie, when she came to the house in Rope Walk, had known perfectly well that Tancred hadn't taken the letter in outrage at Hay's immorality. She had felt guilty because her carelessness in leaving the letter for Tancred to find meant that Oscar Hay's plans, with which she was supposed to be helping him, would be circumvented. She wanted Charter to help but she knew he would only do so if she herself were involved so she pretended it was the love aspect of the letter that interested Tancred. In fact he'd only wanted the letter because of the part which mocked the Prime Minister.

A threat to show such a letter to the Prime Minister might stop Hay in his tracks and put an end to his campaign to punish the surgeon for the death of his child.

He frowned. It still wouldn't do. He felt he was beginning to understand Gurth Tancred and was in fact becoming rather fond of the man. Using the letter to save his career was blackmail — however you looked at it. Was Tancred that sort of man?

And then it occurred to him that Tancred might have had a perfectly respectable motive. He might simply have wanted to protect Sophie from Oscar Hay's advances. So romantically inclined a man was probably a little in love with Sophie himself. Men did tend to fall in love with Sophie. And, if so, he might have felt the same revulsion Charter himself felt at the thought of Sophie and Hay together.

And then Charter saw beyond this to another perfectly possible motive. Tancred must have got to know the

Hay family during the time the little girl was having treatment at St Christopher's. In those circumstances you get to know the surgeon, Hay had said. Tancred may have liked Hay's wife. He must have felt Hay's behaviour over Sophie was outrageous in the circumstances. He might simply have wanted to use the letter to save the Hay marriage. And Sophie might have been merely incidental to that.

He began carefully to go over everything Sophie had told him about her relationship with Hay. He got up, stretched luxuriously and began to walk round the room. And, as he did, much became clear to him.

Sophie's story was completely wrong psychologically. He pictured Sophie as she had talked to him about Hay. The story had shocked him so much that it had taken him off guard. Sophie had been wearing that wide-eyed look of hers that meant mischief. What had she said? Hay had told her she was magic, plied her with champagne and lured her to bed with him at Bray. Sophie had asked Charter to believe that, after this event, Hay had become besotted with her and it was only then that he started sending her streams of love letters. But the letters he had found in Sophie's bedroom were the letters of a suppliant, not of a lover assuaged. And Oscar Hay, unless Charter was wrong, was the sort of man for whom the chase was all important. The thing that would drive a man of his stamp to behave like a lovelorn swain would be failure to attain his goal, not success.

And how did this discovery affect the investigation? It meant that Hay would still have been regarding Tancred as a rival. It was already evident that he was jealous of Sophie's friendship with Tancred. He may also have suspected that she was becoming less eager to help him with the exposé of Tancred and St Christopher's. This would make him even more angry with Tancred. Tancred had charmed Sophie into what Hay would regard as disloyalty to him, a disinclination to go on with the investigation. And, knowing Sophie as well as he did, Charter thought it probable that she would have told

Hay as soon as she decided that she didn't care for what he was trying to do. On top of that Hay could well have suspected that Tancred had succeeded in seducing Sophie. A fairly strong set of motives reinforcing his antagonism to Tancred.

But all this provided good reason too for Hay to feel hostile to Sophie and on more than one count. It was beginning to look as if Hay had a sound enough motive for anger against Tancred and could well have entered into an argument with him on the lane that led to his home, an argument that ended in a struggle and a sudden lethal blow. His heart began to beat hard against his ribs as he saw the corollary to that which was that if Hay had killed Tancred he had probably killed Sophie too.

Although he knew that all this was the wildest speculation he could not persuade himself that Sophie was not indeed lost and gone.

He decided to collect the sergeant and go and talk to Miss Fisher who would know, if anyone knew, the rights and wrongs of the death of Caroline Hay.

But even as he made this decision he felt more strongly than ever that this was a nightmare and a nightmare that would go on until it had engulfed him and Sophie and the children.

10

The Senior Nursing Officer

MISS FISHER answered the door herself. She was good-looking, about forty, tall, thin and wiry, a little over made-up. She had large brown eyes and a wide smile that was full of kindness and good humour. "I've already been interviewed, you know, but do come in and sit down," she said and took them into a drawing-room which was slightly frilly in some respects and distinctly workmanlike in others. "Won't you and the sergeant have a drink?" she asked.

"No thank you. Yours must be a very responsible job. I suppose part at least of the function of the old Gorgon matrons must be vested in you."

"I do hope I'm not a Gorgon, but you're quite right. I'm the admin bit. Hardly do any nursing nowadays, more's the pity. But I'm sure you didn't come here to talk about hospital administration."

"No. I wonder whether you can think of any reason for anyone to murder your professor."

"No, I can't. That's why everybody says it must have been a tramp or a madman and the girls are all terrified to go out at night."

"Was the professor well liked?"

"Yes, he was. And people felt sorry for him too. Myra Tancred's a complete neurotic. He was very good to her."

"How good a surgeon was he?"

"He was brilliant. He knew when not to operate. You'd be surprised how many operations are done simply to keep the patient quiet. And some surgeons are bored with everything except the high tech ops. Gurth Tancred wasn't like that. He did operations for the good of his patients. He never considered the reputation of this hospital. That was an attitude that really got up the nose of our Mr Jackson, the administrator. The reputation of St Christopher's is the only thing on earth that matters to him. Once Gurth made up his mind on what was the right thing to do for the patient, he wouldn't budge. They could beg him to operate until they were blue in the face. He wouldn't do it."

"Didn't that cause resentment?"

"Oh no. The patients love it. But if he thought there was the slightest chance he would always operate if that was what the patient and the family wanted. Not all surgeons will do that. Surgeons don't like deaths on the table. It's bad for their reputation."

"So Professor Tancred was one of the best surgeons. Were the others jealous of his success?"

"They're all pretty successful themselves. I don't think they really have the time to go in for emotional reactions like that. They're usually rushed off their feet. Have you ever seen a surgical team at work in an emergency? It'd surprise you. I don't know how they keep their sanity."

"Perhaps they don't."

"I'd know if that were so. I don't think there's any solution that way. I'm sure we haven't any real nutters here. Though it's true that men can be very silly about success and failure. They get so uptight about who has the most important job and the biggest car."

"But surely success must have become rather important to you too."

"You're trying to catch me out! I've had to fight very hard for what I've achieved and don't you forget it. Of course I'm glad to have done so well and I've got a lovely Renault but I sometimes wish I was a ward sister again. It's nothing but admin, and never seeing a patient. I feel I'm never going to be at the sharp end again. Success is nice but you have to pay for it."

"Did Professor Tancred have to pay for it?"

"I should think he probably did. For one thing his wife might not have got so peculiar if he'd had more time for her. He used to give her everything that opens and shuts — furnished the house regardless to make her happy. But it was no good. She got drearier and drearier and more and more miserable."

"Now, Miss Fisher, did you know that the professor was a Freemason?"

"Yes, I did. Silly man."

"You don't approve of the Brotherhood?"

"Of course I don't. All that dressing-up and swearing silly oaths. And the stag nights and the blue films. Disgusting I call it. And it's all so undignified. I couldn't really respect a man who got seriously involved with that lot."

"So you didn't respect the professor."

She considered this, her head on one side, then said reluctantly, "Well, I don't like to admit it but over the last few years I've come to feel rather sad about him. I suppose I did lose some of my respect for him. But I did love him. He was so good and kind and so understanding with that awful wife of his. So marvellous with his patients. And he wasn't the slightest bit of a money grabber like some of them are. He just got on with it and did the best he could for his patients."

"I believe he went in for one or two lady friends over the last year or two."

"Yes. He started losing his head over young women. I don't think it ever went very far. He always went home to Myra but he got a bit silly about them."

"Do you think Dr Parchment resented his affair with Dr Prideaux?"

"Of course not." Then she smiled. "Well, to be honest, yes, I suppose he did a bit, as he got engaged to her as soon as Prof gave her the push."

"It was Prof gave her the push, was it?"

"Oh yes. She was heart-broken. Still is, if you ask me. William Parchment was just any port in a storm and I'm sure he knew it."

"Could he have been jealous enough to kill the professor in a sudden fit of fury?"

"Oh how can you? That nice boy! Of course he couldn't. That clever boy, I should say."

"Did the professor hold the young men back by refusing to delegate?"

"Of course not. He brought them on at their own pace."

"Did he have some failures?"

"Failed ops, do you mean? Well, of course. We're not infallible, you know."

"Miss Fisher," he said, "I want to put a hypothetical case to you. Supposing you began to suspect that one of the senior consultants at St Christopher's was turning up at a small percentage of his operations very slightly the worse for drink. What steps would you take?"

Her face froze for two seconds then she was answering the question calmly and authoritatively. He began to see what had brought her so responsible a job.

"Well, the correct thing to do would be to report my suspicions to the hospital administrator."

"And that's what you would do?"

"Yes, once I'd checked I'd have to take it to him."

"And what action would the administrator take?"

"It would be a very difficult decision for him. Being in theatre even slightly under the influence would amount to gross misconduct on the part of a surgeon. Jackson would have to discuss the whole thing with Gurth's senior colleagues and there would have to be a full investigation. It would be a real headache. You could hardly get a top consultant to blow into a breathalizer and I'd like to see his face if anyone asked him to supply blood or urine samples. So how could you prove he was drunk? And he would certainly appeal and he wouldn't be drunk when he was hauled before the tribunal, would he? He'd be his usual sensible competent and authoritative self. So no one would believe the administrator. They'd acquit Gurth and Bob would look a fool."

"What do you know about Oscar Hay's little daughter?" he asked suddenly. She looked away and he was surprised to see that she was blushing.

Some people, he thought, blush when they lie. Is she going to lie now?

"It was a very sad case," she said. "I'd much rather not talk about it."

"Miss Fisher," he said. "I'd much rather not talk about any of this. But it's my duty and it's yours, so let's get on with it. Was Prof to blame?"

"You can't do more than your best."

"I'm told the parents were resentful and blamed the professor."

"People go a bit over the top in the circumstances."

"Were they planning to sue?"

"They talked about it but it would have come to nothing."

"So you don't think Oscar Hay and the Prof were locked in mortal combat over the failed operation on Caroline Hay?"

"My goodness, so you do really think Oscar Hay had Prof murdered?"

"Had him murdered? Why do you say that?"

"Well, he could hardly have done it himself here at the hospital. Don't forget, he and his wife were coming here for weeks. We all knew them. He couldn't possibly have hoped to get away with it."

"On a dark evening in the rain? Wearing a mackintosh with the collar and hood up and a rainhat pulled well down? Anyone could have got away with it."

"Oh my goodness! Oscar Hay. But he's sure to have an alibi. MPs are always surrounded by official people. And surely he would be too intelligent to think of killing the surgeon because the op went wrong. You can never guarantee the success of any operation. Complications can arise quite unexpectedly."

"Not everyone can behave logically when emotionally involved."

"No. And she was a darling little girl. It almost broke up their marriage. They got to resent each other You could see it happening. I'm afraid that often happens.

109

But they do get over it in the end. Well, sometimes they do. They say they still lead completely separate lives."

"But in the end they decided not to sue?"

"What would be the point? Who would testify against Prof in this hospital? Not that there was anything to testify about."

"I see. I believe there are several Freemasons in the hospital. I suppose they would close ranks in defence of their high official."

"Prof, you mean? I suppose they might but it wouldn't make any difference. All the medics would close ranks for Prof. Or any other colleague in difficulties, Mason or not."

"So he was in difficulties?"

"Yes. No. I don't know."

"So he did make a mess of the operation."

"I tell you, he was the best surgeon we're ever likely to see here. You're barking up the wrong tree. You really are."

"Very well, Miss Fisher. Now, Detective Sergeant Cobbold will take your statement. We have to establish where everyone was at the time of the murder."

"As a matter of fact I was here all evening. And I didn't see a soul or make a single phone call, which is very unusual for me. I'm usually on the blower non-stop in the evenings. But I was writing an article for *Nursing Times* and the time flew past. I suppose, living in the lane, I could be one of your chief suspects."

"There is the question of motive. There must be any number of people with the opportunity."

"Oh dear, I hadn't thought of that." A look of great dismay came over the open ingenuous face. "Then our nurses are being just a little bit illogical in being afraid to go out at night. The danger could be right here in the hospital."

"If there is a danger. It was probably someone with a grudge against the professor. That doesn't mean he would necessarily want to harm anyone else."

"It's not a very nice feeling all the same. I think I'll ask one of the ward sisters to come and sleep here until this is all over." She looked about her nervously.

"I should do that if I were you. I

don't think you are in any danger but a companion would be reassuring if you woke up in the middle of the night and felt nervous."

She gave a little scream. "Don't say that!" she said and showed them out without a trace of the sunny smile.

They walked away down to the hospital.

"What did you make of that, Derek?" asked Charter.

"She was protesting too much over the professor," said Cobbold, and Charter nodded.

"Yes," he said. "Something was going on. The man was obviously extremely competent. Then he must have been drunk or on drugs or ill or indulging in sexual activity to an abnormal extent."

11

Mr Jackson Stonewalls

THEY walked at a great pace across to the Jackson house. Mr Jackson was still drinking coffee when the bell rang and he came out holding a napkin round his right hand.

"Just a moment," he said, "I've just scalded my hand with the kettle. Go into the sitting-room. I'll just run some cold water on it."

He came back a minute or two later.

"Good morning," he said curtly. "What can I do for you this time?"

"This time," said Charter, "you can tell me what makes everyone in this hospital so embarrassed when the subject of Professor Tancred's operations comes up. I'm quite convinced that the cause of his murder is connected with that. I want the truth now, Mr Jackson. What was it — incompetence, drunkenness?"

Mr Jackson stared back at him, red

113

in the face. Then his eyes flickered and looked away. "Nothing of the kind," he said.

"Mr Jackson, there is no possible way you can protect St Christopher's from scandal now that your professor has been bludgeoned to death. If I can solve this crime quickly, say, today, there'll be a furore but it will be over all the sooner. So tell me everything now. If not, we're going to have to go through all your medical records to dig it up."

Jackson glanced up at him and looked away again.

"Ah, I see. You've taken care of the records. Then we'll have to talk to the entire staff — doctors, nurses, NUPE workers, patients and the patients' families. It will take much longer but we'll get there in the end."

"Where? I don't know what you're talking about. I've told you, Professor Tancred was a brilliant surgeon and a most respected man. There is nothing questionable or scandalous involving anyone in this hospital."

"What about Tancred's failed operations?"

Jackson exploded with fury. "Who said

he had any failed operations? If he were still alive that would be slander and I'd have you reprimanded for it. He was one of the most distinguished surgeons in the country. These rumours are very damaging and I shall get to the bottom of them and sack the people who are talking so carelessly. They could ruin this hospital and the unit at Penchester. And so could you. I hope you are aware of it."

"I'll bear it in mind. Thank you for your help, sir. Now, would you be so good as to show me your hand. The one you scalded before we came."

Jackson held it out to him without a word. There was no bruising of the knuckles just an inflamed area around the thumb and forefinger.

"Thank you, sir," said Charter.

He turned and walked away, the sergeant at his heels.

"Now for Mrs Tancred," he said, and went into a sprint followed by the sergeant. After a long interval Myra Tancred opened the door. She was wearing a frilly dressing-gown and fluffy pink mules. Her hair was loose on her shoulders and uncombed. Her eyes were swollen and reddened and the skin below the eyes and round the mouth looked as if she had cried for hours.

"I'm sorry to call so early," he began, and she said quickly, "It doesn't matter. I am usually up before six." She led them into the drawing-room. The curtains were still drawn, the ashes lay in the hearth, and two mugs stood on the tiles within the fender. Myra sat down with her head bent, her shoulders sagging.

"Mrs Tancred," he said gently, "I've come to ask you about your husband's reputation as a surgeon. Can you help me about that? Was he in some sort of trouble?"

She looked up at him then lowered her head again and shook it.

"I am beginning to believe," he told her, "that there were some incidents in his otherwise brilliant career which may have caused some patients to question his performance as a surgeon on some occasions. I can't find out anything about it at the hospital because they are all being foolishly discreet, as doctors often are to protect the reputation of their

116

colleagues. Did your husband sometimes drink too much when he was on duty?"

"It's nothing to do with that," she said.

"So there was something?"

"I don't know anything about it."

"Miss Fisher and Mr Jackson know something about it. I can't believe that you've heard no gossip in the hospital."

"You'll have to believe it," she said. "He never talked to me about his work. And I have nothing to do with the hospital."

"Surely, as wife of the senior surgeon, you must have attended functions?"

"I don't. I stopped all that years ago. They don't like me at the hospital. He did sometimes drink too much at home."

"I see. Well, if anything occurs to you which might help us will you let me know? Here's the number of the police station."

"Thank you."

"Are you in some particular distress this morning, Mrs Tancred? Can I be of any help?"

"No. Not now." She came out to the

door with them and let them out.

"Something very wrong there," he said to the sergeant. "I wonder whether that young woman is playing up."

"You don't think it could be remorse, sir?"

"No, Sergeant, I don't think she killed her husband. I think we'd better check up on the young woman. If she ran out on her it would explain the tears."

They walked briskly down the lane and through the courtyard into the hospital.

"Ann Prideaux," said Charter. "We'll get some sense out of her."

12

Ann Prideaux

THEY found her in her room and this time she was once again with a companion in a white coat. She and Doctor Parchment were locked in each other's arms. William Parchment had his back to them and they could see Dr Prideaux' long fingers stroking and caressing his neck and running through the tight curls on the well-shaped head.

As they broke away from each other and swung round, they both looked surprised but neither seemed embarrassed.

"I apologize," said Charter, "for coming in at the wrong moment. I'm afraid I have to ask you to leave Dr Prideaux with us for a few minutes, Dr Parchment?"

"Gladly," said Parchment. "Farewell, my lovely. The canteen at one."

She leaned forward to cling to his hand until he was at the door. Then she let him go and turned to the policemen.

"Sorry," she said. "Do sit down."

They did so and she drifted round the desk and stood there smiling at them vaguely.

Charter was brisk. "Dr Prideaux," he said, "I think Professor Tancred may have been killed because of some question about his competence as a surgeon. I need the facts about any problems which may have arisen in the surgical department of this hospital."

She sat down at the desk and folded her hands. "You're wrong," she said. "You can take it from me that if there were any rumours of that kind there is absolutely no substance in them. Gurth Tancred was a first-class surgeon and he was absolutely correct."

"What about Oscar Hay's child?"

"A very unfortunate case. There was nothing to be done. The parents were warned that there was only an outside chance she could be saved. The parents talked about suing but they wouldn't have gone through with it."

"So you don't think he could have been murdered for any reason connected with a failure as a surgeon?"

"Gurth had failings as a man but as a surgeon he was the best."

"Thank you," said Charter. "Now we have your statement about your movements the day before yesterday. You saw no strangers loitering about the hospital, particularly towards evening?"

"No. I was working in here. I ate in the canteen. I was here until I was called down to the mortuary to assist Mr Harvey Knott."

"But you were in your room when we came."

"Yes. He changed his mind when he saw how upset I was and called someone else. He's a pompous old ass but he's quite kind when it comes to the point."

★ ★ ★

As they took the lift, Charter said, "I wonder whether this is another example of the solidarity of the medical profession in the face of hints about malpractice. I don't think so. And this time there are certainly no Masonic overtones. She can't be acting on instructions from the Brethren."

121

"Unless she were under the influence of one of them."

"Tancred was a Mason but Parchment says he isn't."

They walked into the front courtyard of the hospital and Charter turned through a gate into the parkland. He looked at the sergeant consideringly. "Sergeant," he said, "I'm going to let you into a secret about this case. It's potentially embarrassing and it's strictly between you and me. If you are the man I think you are you'll be able to handle that. But, if you prefer it, I'll take you off the case."

The sergeant regarded him woodenly. "No sir," he said.

Charter smiled. "It's tricky," he said, "and it means that I've got to get through this case like a knife through butter. That ought to give you some scope.

"On the evening when this case broke, but before I knew anything about it, a young woman called Sophie Saltram came to see me. Until a little over a year ago she was my wife. She has always been fairly widely known as Sophie Saltram because she is a photographer and for those purposes she retained her maiden name." Charter told the sergeant the story and then said, "Now it seems to me that Professor Tancred is almost certainly the man."

"Sounds like it, sir," said the sergeant.

"But it doesn't fit, Derek," said Charter. "You've heard what they all say about Tancred. Kindly, rumpled, falls romantically in love. Won't hurt his wife's feelings if he can help it. Retires gracefully when Dr Prideaux gives him his *congé*. Rejoices in the success of his protégés. And has an affair with the au pair girl. Does that sound like a man who would steal a letter and use it for blackmail because he's against immorality in an MP though he's quite ready to indulge in it himself? I just don't believe it. Unless they are all lying about him."

"Can't you ask Miss Saltram, sir?"

Charter gave him a long look then said, "No, I can't. Miss Saltram has disappeared. If it weren't for that fact I might now retire from this case. I believe I can find Miss Saltram faster than anyone else can and I will then learn from her the whole story. I shall go to see the ACC as soon as I can get an appointment, to give him the story. I'm sure you see the ramifications of that."

"With a Member of Parliament? Yes, sir. It may be a matter for Special Branch."

"It may well. I expect to get a day or two's grace from the ACC. No more. So we're in a hurry, Sergeant. I reckon to solve this one within two days. It's clear that our most likely suspect at this stage is Oscar Hay. And there is a chance that Sophie is involved with him, though it's unlikely. But, if she is involved against him, then he may have — dealt with that, in some way I don't care to contemplate."

"I'm very sorry, sir," said the sergeant. "I'll do what I can twenty-four hours a day if it's needed."

"Thank you, Derek. It's all the merest speculation at present. We've got to get the evidence."

After this, Charter called in at the Incident Room and gave a short TV interview, trying unsuccessfully to conceal his impatience at what he considered to be a complete waste of his time. This

124

was a job for the PR people. Not for a busy detective.

For some reason the public had latched on to this attitude and they found it amusing. So, instead of having the reputation he deserved of being a rather bad-tempered, brusque CID man on TV, he had become a popular figure and was known ironically as 'Chatty Charter'.

13

The City

IN desperation Charter now drove up to London to call on Hartley Godwin. Hartley had become a close friend more perhaps of Sophie than himself. She sometimes went over to Hangholt Manor to exercise his hunters. Charter cherished a forlorn hope that Sophie might have told Hartley where she was going and why.

The unrelenting rain was back again, misty and fine, drifting in the headlights, coating the surface of the road with a glimmering sheen. Heavy chalk-white clouds hung above the City drooping lower as the day wore on and gradually darkening through grey and umber to a purplish black.

He rang the bell at Pinbolt House, a block of flats in Pin Lane. A deep, pleasant, mid-Atlantic voice came through the loud speaker.

126

"Hartley Godwin here. Yes?"

"John Charter."

"John! Come up at once!"

And it was with a welcoming smile that he threw open his door a few minutes later.

Charter walked into the huge, bright room with the raindrop covered window of small square panes stretching along the whole length of the long room and giving it the appearance of the captain's cabin in a ship of the line. This impression was strengthened by the view of the river at dusk edged with the glow at regular intervals of the street lamps and patterned with a scatter of red, green and white lights from river craft.

"Well," said Hartley, "so at last you come to see me. I must have been at least a dozen times to you."

"Nice flat," said Charter. "I'd have come long ago but you know how little time I have and there are the children and Sophie."

"You see Sophie regularly then?"

"No. We don't have any arrangement about that. I see her when she feels disposed to see me. But I have a regular

127

arrangement for having Robert and India for a whole day once a fortnight and in practice I see them oftener than that."

Hartley poured whiskey from a collection of decanters.

They sat down. "I like your Stubbs," said Charter. "I expected a Stubbs."

"It's not Stubbs," said Hartley. "It's a pupil of his called John Boultbee. A good painter but not so well known."

"Hartley," said John, "I've lost Sophie. She's vanished into thin air and I'm quietly going mad."

"Do you want to tell me about it?"

Charter told him.

"It sounds," said Hartley, "like Sophie taking a breather on something she wants to think about on her own. Perhaps she got hold of some special knowledge about the murder."

"If it's special knowledge about that it could be dangerous."

"She'd surely realize that. Sophie's no fool. And, though she doesn't look it, she's as strong as a horse. It wouldn't be at all easy to 'disappear' Sophie without trace. I'm convinced she's all right."

John looked at him very hard and went

away almost convinced that Hartley knew something. He felt relieved and hurt and angry and, at the same time, he knew perfectly well that he had no grounds whatsoever for this belief. Hartley was his friend. If he knew where Sophie was, surely he would have told. No. He wouldn't have told then and there because he would have to consult Sophie. So a call might conceivably come that evening, either from Sophie herself, or from Hartley. But no calls came to Rope Walk that evening and the feeling of nightmare grew. At nine o'clock he put on his mackintosh and his tweed hat and went out leaving the answer phone on. He would check William Parchment's alibi with the charlady at the sports centre.

14

Lily

LILY was on her hands and knees energetically scrubbing the linoleum floor. She turned to wring out the cloth after dipping her chapped red hands into the pail beside her and looked up at him over her shoulder. Her red-rimmed, rheumy old eyes snapped with pleasure.

"You're the fuzz," she told him firmly.

"And it's a long time since I saw anyone giving a floor such a thorough cleaning," said Charter admiringly.

A pleased smile creased the wrinkled face. "The young 'uns wouldn't never do it," she said. "Spray like mad, give it the once over with the polisher and that's yer lot. Never mind the corners and under the furniture. Then before you can blink an eye you've got the build-up."

Charter was visited by inspiration.

"May I share a pot of tea with you

while I ask you a few questions?"

"What sort of questions?" she asked suspiciously.

"Quite straightforward ones about where everybody was the night the professor was murdered."

"Well I reckon that can't do no harm. You get sat down on that sofa over there while I brew up the tea."

After banging about in the kitchen noisily for a while she came back with a pot of tea, and a plate of digestive biscuits.

"Don't stint yourself," she said. "Take a digestive. Do you good. This time of night I reckon you need fortifying."

"You're an angel, Mrs — "

"Lily. I don't get nothing but Lily. Wouldn't recernize meself by nothing else. I'll be mother."

She put heaped spoonfuls of sugar in both cups before he could stop her and settled back in her chair stretching out her feet with a groan.

"Did anyone come into the sports centre that night?"

"Only Dr Parchment," she said. "He comes down to have a nap of an evening.

Poor boy. He comes in and flings hisself down on the couch in there. I don't know what she'd say if she knew but the poor boy needs his sleep. I just gets on with it and when I'm finished I makes him a nice pot of tea with a digestive and off he goes."

"He doesn't have a key then? He has to leave when you leave?"

"Well I'm in charge an' all. Anything goes missing I'd be the one, wouldn't I?"

"But he comes in when he wants to? He doesn't have to ring the bell? You leave the door open?"

"And why not? We're part of the hospital, aren't we? We're quite safe in the hospital."

"I see. Could Dr Parchment have got out of the sports centre without your seeing him?"

"What, that lovely boy murder the professor? That's a laugh, that is. And he couldn't have anyway because I was working outside the door of the aroma whatnot room all evening and didn't budge. So how could he?"

"So you took the tea in to him later

on in the evening when you were about to go home?"

"That's right. Eleven o'clock. And there he was sleeping like a baby. Never moved since nine o'clock."

"Well that's good, Lily. If you're quite sure of this you've given Dr Parchment an alibi. If he was here from nine till eleven he couldn't possibly have been out in the lane hitting the professor over the head."

"Of course he couldn't. Aren't I telling you?"

"And no one came down to see him?"

"I didn't see no one."

"Aren't there any windows down here?"

"Not a one. Well it stands to reason. It's the basement."

"Thank you, Lily. You've been a great help."

He drove home carefully, forcing himself not to allow the car to gather speed, and walked to the answer phone. There was no message. He made a mental note that Sergeant Cobbold should have a look round the sports centre in the morning to check how water-tight Dr

Parchment's alibi might be. He went to bed and tossed and turned, drifting off to sleep for a few minutes then waking up in a cold sweat, then getting up to make coffee and sit a while by the Aga before returning to bed and lying despondently awake.

15

The Break-In

IT was half past two when the call came from Cathy. Her voice came over the phone in a terrified whisper and he caught his breath.

"Mr Charter. It's Cathy. There's someone in the house. He's been moving about in your wife's room."

"Which room are you in, Cathy?"

"The nursery. I've put the bolt on."

"Good girl. Don't be frightened. I'll get someone to you and I'll be there soon after. Put a chair-back under the door knob. That'll make doubly sure. But he's looking for something. It won't be anything to do with the children."

The nursery wing of Mill House had been a granny flat when the former owners were in charge. They should be safe in there.

On the road to Mill House the speedometer rarely fell below seventy.

The wind drove the rain towards the windscreen and the wipers sloshed it blindingly to and fro. The Rover streaked along, driven with fierce precision. Every so often as the car went through a dip in the road the wheels flung up a wave of water.

All the windows of Mill House were lighted up. Two uniformed men were measuring tyre tracks in the drive. A uniformed sergeant met him in the hall.

"He must have heard her put down the receiver, sir. He's scarpered. The girl heard the tyres screech as he reversed at speed. We've put out a call but we don't know what car it is. Other than the size. They're all all right, sir. We've got them in here." He took Charter into the drawing-room.

A red-eyed Cathy was smiling bravely with her arms round the sleepy children.

He kissed all three and took both Cathy's hands in his.

"Cathy, I'm sorry," he said. "Where's Clarissa?"

"She had to go home. She'll be back first thing. Her cat had kittens and the lady who keeps an eye on things for her was away for the night."

"Well I'm sorry you had such a fright. I'll get you all out of here at once."

Her lip trembled. "Where can we go? There's Robert's school."

"Never mind school. It won't hurt him to miss a day or two. You're coming home with me. I'll run you over to Clarissa's first thing in the morning."

The children danced upstairs, holding on to his hands and made a great to-do about choosing toys to take with them. Then he bundled them into the car, still in their slippers and dressing-gowns, and Flymo, the Sealyham, jumped in after them.

The sergeant came over to the car.

"He's turned the room over pretty thoroughly, sir."

"He did, did he? Well, I know what he was looking for and he was wasting his time. We've already got it under wraps at the station."

Underneath the deference there was an air of suppressed excitement. It was no doubt intriguing to work on a case with a Super whose wife and family were involved.

137

Even Cathy was beaming with pleasure and excitement as he bundled them up the steps and into the house on Rope Walk.

The children ran round the room looking at everything.

"That's Mummy," said Robert, picking up a photograph of Sophie flat on her stomach on a sea wall in sou'wester and oil skins waving an arm gaily against a background of cloud and spray.

Charter led Cathy up to the spare room.

"Straight to bed," he said. "I'll send Robert up in a minute with a hot drink and a hot water bottle."

The children sipped their mugs of chocolate beside the warmth of the Aga while he made up beds on the floor. He tucked them up, then lay down on the sofa in his track suit and they all slept until seven. Then he telephoned Clarissa and she answered in a high hoarse croak.

"Oh God," she said. "How could I have left them? But it never entered my head that anything like that could happen. Cathy's so responsible. I'm so sorry, John.

138

And now I've got a temperature and I feel frightfully ill. I don't want to give it to the children. Do you think Cathy could cope for a day or two?"

"She'll do very well," he said. "I'll keep them here. But after this I can't let Cathy stop there alone even in the daytime."

"Why don't you move into Mill House with them?"

"It's a nice idea but it's Sophie's house now, not mine. I gave it to her when I left. Remember?"

"That's irrelevant in the circumstances."

"Not to me. But in any case I can't be sure of being there even at night."

"Keep them at Rope Walk for a day or two then. I'll be better soon."

"Look after yourself then, Clarissa. I'll keep you posted. We're looking for Sophie now for real. We'll soon find where she is. Don't worry."

16

The ACC

AT 7.45 that morning Charter and Godfrey Baldwin were sitting at the Baldwins' kitchen table with coffee and croissants, facing the window with the famous view of the cathedral.

Godfrey Baldwin was sixty-two, overweight but fighting fit. He was completely trustworthy and kind. Charter knew him very well by now and he thanked his gods that this was the man who must decide whether to let him go on with the case.

"Well?" said the ACC.

"It's a stinker," said Charter. "I had to disturb you at this hour because we may have to change the team. You may have to throw me out. Technically I should probably take myself off the case. There is an outside chance that my former wife is involved at the periphery."

"What has Sophie been up to?"

140

Charter told him. The ACC's frown got deeper. From time to time he shook his head to indicate dismay.

"I've no control over Sophie now," Charter explained.

"You never did have any control over her, my dear John. That was the trouble."

"Well as I see it, if the problem with the letter was the fact that it is a fairly explicit love letter to a particular woman revealing the peccadilloes of a prospective cabinet minister, then I'd have to come off the case at once. Then Sophie's behaviour would have a direct influence on the case. But as Hay thought the rudery to the PM was the part of the letter which could do him damage I reckon that gets me off the hook. Sophie's behaviour becomes irrelevant. The letter could have been addressed to anyone and the fact that it was addressed to Sophie has no relevance to the murder."

"It's pretty dicey, John."

"I know it is but if I can solve it fast it'll be all right. If I don't you can take me off it."

"You don't in fact believe that Oscar Hay could have killed him to stop him from sending the letter to the PM?"

"I've no specific theory as yet. I think that letter would be curtains for Hay as minister. But there are several other lines of inquiry. The thing is, no one is going to get anywhere as fast as I am. I know a lot of the people. I know Sophie."

"Where is she? I'd like a word with her."

"Sorry. Impossible. She dashed out into the night when the call came for me and she's disappeared into thin air."

The ACC looked concerned. "That's worrying," he said.

"A message came to the nanny explaining that Sophie's gone off to work on a film but someone else phoned the message through."

"Where's her car?"

"Gone too."

"You'd better put a call out for it at once."

"Thank you, I shall. She'll be furious if she is peacefully working on a film set but I don't think she is. We have to consider the possibility that she went from me to see Gurth Tancred at his house. You get to it through the hospital and along the lane where the body was found. By the time she got there the scene-of-crime lads had taken over. She wouldn't have got through. But she might have run into the murderer somewhere in the area of the hospital. He might have thought he had betrayed himself. Perhaps his clothes were bloodstained. Perhaps it was obvious that there was no good reason for him to be there. Perhaps he showed some distress that she would be likely to remember against him in the witness box. I have to face the fact that he may have kidnapped her. Or killed her."

At last he had said it. No feeling of shock as the words fell into a sudden sharp silence. Just a sort of lethargy out of which his voice continued in a careful monotone. "One is obliged to consider that possibility. I admit that normally if it became apparent that my former wife might figure as victim in a murder investigation I should be removed from the case at once. But I submit that no one else has a hope in hell of solving this case as fast as I can. For one thing I have some useful information on Oscar Hay."

He handed over a transcript of the conversation of the previous evening. The ACC glanced down at it and his frown became even blacker. "Good God, John! You can't have gone to Oscar Hay."

"No, sir. He telephoned and asked me to listen to what he had to say. Then he came to see me at my house. He asked me to keep the meeting secret. I told him that was impossible. In fact the only circumstances in which I could have done that would have been if I decided to leave the Force and carry on the investigation on my own."

"It won't come to that."

He read the document through, looking up at Charter from time to time and shaking his head.

"I don't know what the guv'nors would say to this, John."

"They don't have to know anything about it till we've solved it. Sophie's disappearance is probably completely innocent. And, in fact, Hay is involved in a completely different way with Tancred.

Nothing to do with Sophie."

"How's that?"

"Professor Tancred operated on Oscar Hay's young daughter. The child died. There may be something in that. Sophie may be able to give us some answers. But you know what a difficult proposition Sophie can be. If anyone can get anything out of her it will be me. Once, of course, we've found her. Another point in my favour is that I've established a relationship with Oscar Hay. Having talked about his problems to me he isn't going to want to talk to sundry other detectives."

"I'm amazed, as you're Sophie's husband, that he has the face to talk to you at all."

"He doesn't know I'm her husband."

"How's that?"

"She told him I'm her brother."

The ACC gave a shout of laughter. "Good God," he said, "I rather envy you your Sophie. So she's guarding your back."

"For the time being."

"And the man believes it?"

"I think so. I was careful not to lead

him astray. I referred simply to 'Sophie' not my 'sister'."

"Well, John, we'll have to work very closely together on this one. I'll want reports in, every hour on the hour."

"When it's humanly possible I'll check everything with you. We have one lead. Last night someone broke into Mill House, stole nothing, damaged nothing, simply went to Sophie's room and rummaged about. The chances are that he was looking for the TV treatment Sophie was researching to help destroy Professor Tancred's career. I reckon it must have been Hay if it wasn't Sophie. Only Hay would know of its existence. Sophie might, of course, have told someone else in the hospital, so if the murderer is one of the hospital staff it could have been him."

"It's all circumstantial, John. I doubt if the DPP would have anything to do with it at this stage but you're certainly building a case against the man. Now what we need is hard evidence."

"That's what I'm going after now."

"Right. I'll give you twenty four hours. If we've made no progress that's it. If it's looking promising you get another twenty four. Then, no matter what, we go to the Chief Constable."

"What about putting Hay under surveillance? I can't be sure he hasn't got Sophie."

"In his house with his family?"

"It's an outside chance but I'd like to make sure."

"Well, Sophie's known as Sophie Saltram these days, isn't she? Not Sophie Charter. For twenty-four hours then. You'll have to use a surveillance team from the Met. I don't suppose there'll be any difficulty about that. We'd better avoid the Regional Crime Squad boys until we're in the open about Sophie."

"Right, sir. I'll get on with it."

"Do that. I don't see that we're going to have any joy from the lab at all on this case and we can sort through criminal records till kingdom come. I don't see a vagrant or a psycho wiping the man out so conveniently. So we're left with you. For some reason suspects seem to queue up in line to tell you all their most closely guarded secrets."

"We'll get results. I promise you."

"Well I hope they'll be the ones we want. Sophie will turn up as right as rain, I'm sure of it. But you get on to it. Official. All the stops out."

"Thank you, sir."

As he went out to his car the feeling of relief was almost painful.

17

Stumpington

HE walked into the station at Stumpington at nine o'clock and learned that as far as tyre measurements were concerned the car could have been Sophie's or one of any number of makes of small car. Sophie? Creeping round her own house at dead of night to retrieve copies of an article which could do her no harm but might demonstrate that Oscar Hay had a strong motive for silencing Professor Tancred? It didn't read like Sophie. It was something Oscar Hay himself would be much more likely to do. There was a man who would pride himself on bending events to his will and wouldn't mind what risks he took. A picture came to him of Hay walking down that lane with the murder weapon clutched in his upraised arm and a look of deadly purpose on his face. He forced himself to dismiss the fearful image.

Sophie's car on the scene at Mill House wouldn't necessarily demonstrate the presence of Sophie herself. She could have lent the car to Hay or whoever else she was with. It was still not totally ruled out that she was innocently engaged upon her film work, though this became with each succeeding hour less likely. And one couldn't overlook the possibility that Sophie no longer had any control over who used her car because she was either a prisoner or —

Was it possible that she was holed-up in London in a place provided for her by Oscar Hay? And that together they had planned to retrieve the evidence against him in Sophie's notes? Sophie in a love nest provided by that obnoxious character? Not likely. Sophie dead? Better not think about that.

If it wasn't Sophie and it wasn't Oscar Hay, who else could that stealthy intruder have been at dead of night in the Mill? Mr Jackson? Miss Fisher? Ann Prideaux? William Parchment? Mr Harvey Knot? Silke von Treiben? Myra Tancred?

Charter collected DCI Cartwright and asked to be taken to his office. There he told him the full story of Oscar Hay, Sophie Saltram, Gurth Tancred and the relationships between them.

Cartwright struggled to hide his embarrassment. He knew perfectly well who Sophie Saltram was. Charter decided not to refer to this complication, but his opinion of Cartwright plummeted.

He told the DCI, "I'm fairly certain now that this wasn't the work of a psycho or a tramp. Chance played no part in this at all. So you could almost take your lads off the knocker if it weren't for the fact that someone may have seen someone in Stumpington who ought not to have been there that evening. I want to put the fear of God into Oscar Hay. I want you to go up and question him and his wife and household about his movements on the night of the murder. We ought, strictly speaking, to talk to Special Branch but as he isn't a cabinet minister yet we'll forget that. I've checked with a lobbyist that he isn't working on anything remotely sensitive so we won't be treading on their toes."

The chief inspector was goggle eyed. "Sir," he said faintly, "you can't treat a

Member of Parliament as if he was just anybody."

"A Member of Parliament is just exactly as accountable to the law of the land as you or I or Joe Bloggs or any member of the Royal family. If he has committed murder he'll be indicted and tried just as we would be. The ACC and I have reviewed the evidence and we believe there's a reasonable case against him."

"Well, if you say so, sir, of course."

Charter said briskly, "We've got a young woman missing in the context of a murder case. That's not a pretty thought. The purloining of the letter by Tancred makes Hay a very possible suspect. I don't care if he's Black Rod himself, I'm not handling him with kid gloves in these circumstances. Of course if he proves to have an unassailable alibi that's a different matter."

"I understand, sir. I'll get up there at once. There was no sign of that letter in Professor Tancred's house or in his room at the hospital."

"Tancred may have sent it back to Hay. Or the murderer may have found

152

it on the body and made off with it. We need to know whether Hay has an alibi. Let me know the answer, pronto."

Again the chief inspector's eye refused to meet his and veered away uncomfortably. Charter's opinion of Cobbold rose in contrast, and rather unfairly, as Cobbold was beginning to know him rather well.

He took leave of the chief inspector and went off to St Christopher's.

His mind was now turning to Myra Tancred who had been so distressed this morning after having shown the day before, such exemplary calm. He walked over to the Tancred house.

Myra answered the door. She looked her old self, tidy in her slacks and pullover, with her hair once again neatly pinned up.

"May I have a word with you, Mrs Tancred?" he asked, and she led him through to the drawing-room. They sat by the fire and he gave her a long look.

"Mrs Tancred," he said, "where is Silke?"

"She's gone."

"Where has she gone?"

"Back to Germany of course. I sent her back."

"Why did you do that? Don't you know that suspects in a murder case are not allowed to leave?"

"You can't suspect a young girl like that."

"I assure you, Mrs Tancred, young girls like that have been known to commit the most atrocious crimes. Age doesn't come into it."

"Oh I see. I shouldn't have let her go then."

"I thought you had planned a life together."

She was silent and the tears were pouring down her cheeks.

"What happened?" he asked gently.

"She just walked out," she said helplessly. "I didn't want anyone to know."

"Mrs Tancred, how long ago did Silke leave? Was it this morning, when we called on you?"

She nodded her head. "When I got up I found her gone. She let herself out with her keys and then she threw them back over the hedge."

"You ought to have told us. We would

154

have had her traced at the airports."

"She had a train and boat ticket. She wouldn't have gone by air. She hadn't much money."

"Then we might have caught up with her and brought her back. Can you give me Silke's address?"

She did so.

"Thank you," he said. "I'll be talking to Hamburg today. I'll let you know whether she arrived safely."

He got up and left and she called to him, "Let me know if you hear anything about that photographer girl. She's a nice girl. Kind and clever. They tell me she's gone too."

He turned back. "Who told you that, Mrs Tancred?"

"The milkman. He had it from the school her little boy goes to. They don't know where she is."

The call to Hamburg was inconclusive. Silke's mother spoke heavily accented but fluent English.

"That's Silke all over," she said, with a laugh. "Silke does what she likes to do. She could be anywhere. She has plenty of friends."

Charter then told her about the murder of the professor.

"What?" she said. "Is that really so? How horrible! Silke must have been very upset."

"Yes. It was unpleasant for her. She found the body."

"That explains it then. Silke doesn't like things that are unpleasant. She doesn't struggle or argue. She just goes away. She has gone away."

Charter rang off, imagining himself and Sophie in years to come reacting to such news about India. He began to feel rather sorry for Silke.

Having set up a full-scale search for the girl he went in to see Myra and tell her that Silke had not returned to Hamburg.

"That other young woman," she said. "Have you heard anything yet? I hope she's still alive. That's two girls missing and there's a murderer about." She spoke in a whisper and Charter's flesh crawled.

"First Gurth," she said, "then Sophie Saltram. And now Silke. Who'll be next?"

18

Dr Porter

CHARTER walked over to the hospital with the sergeant and had Dr Porter bleeped. He came down looking weary but was very polite.

"I'm sorry to call you from your lunch," said Charter, "but this is all very urgent. First, we've learned that Professor Tancred sometimes operated when under the influence of alcohol. Can you tell us anything about that?"

Dr Porter was silent.

"Please answer."

"Well it's not something one would want to bandy about."

"Don't attempt to bandy it about, just answer the question."

"Well then, yes. We had all begun to think that there were occasions when he might have been thought to be a little the worse for wear."

"So did you try to suggest that he might

157

think about refraining from operating on such occasions?"

"Well, no. You couldn't have taken that line with Prof. He was a great man, you know. The decision whether or not to operate could only be his."

"But you must all have been aware that his judgement was gradually becoming affected."

"I expect that's right. But he was the boss."

"And did his operations sometimes end disastrously?"

"No. They were almost always fine. But lately we've had one that ended very badly. That's one too many of course."

"How did it end? With the patient brain-damaged who ought not to have been brain-damaged?"

"No one could make a definite judgement like that. You could only say that he might conceivably have been all right. No one ever knows for certain.. We couldn't find anyone to take him, so he's on a side ward of his own. He sometimes shouts a bit."

"Was Professor Tancred embarrassed about this case?"

"He didn't appear to be. That's the problem with drink. You think you are doing all right. And anyway, so many of our cases are pretty hopeless. The chances are often not more than fifty-fifty and sometimes much worse than that, though, of course, there are some very successful techniques."

"Was the professor worse for drink on the day he operated on Caroline Hay?"

"No. Absolutely not. He did a brilliant job. Unfortunately luck wasn't with us."

"So Oscar Hay was quite wrong in thinking that the Professor was drunk when he operated on their daughter?"

"Of course he wasn't drunk. You don't understand. There was never anything to show that there was anything wrong with Prof. If there had been it would have been easy. He'd have been retired long ago. These suspicions are only just beginning to surface and it's almost impossible for any of us to believe it of Prof. He's been a hero."

"How did Oscar Hay get the idea then?"

"He found out about the patient in the side ward a short time ago. He began to ask questions about Prof. Then he began to think about medical negligence."

"It seems outrageous that nobody tried to stop the man from operating."

"A superb and highly respected surgeon ninety percent of whose operations are performed competently, and sometimes brilliantly?"

"And I suppose you would all close ranks against Hay?"

"Well we knew that on that one Prof was unassailable."

"So any appeal to the General Medical Council would be doomed to failure?"

"I imagine so."

"Will the other family sue?"

"Too early to say. I don't think they're very sophisticated. Hay might decide to champion them. He's obsessed with the whole subject."

"Obsessed enough to have killed Professor Tancred?"

"Surely not. I wouldn't have thought it was that sort of obsession."

"What do you know about Dr Parchment's movements that evening?"

"I didn't see him after eight o'clock. After we'd finished with the crash victims we all staggered off to get some rest. I still rest near the wards but William says it's too noisy for him up there so he goes down to the sports centre. The poor bloke gets really pooped. It's the hours. They're killing. William's shattered. And the affair between Ann and Prof didn't help. William has had his eye on Ann for quite a while. He's going back to Australia one of these days and he wants to take Ann with him. His parents still live out there."

"He doesn't sound like an Australian."

"No. They emigrated when he was fifteen. He came back alone to go to medical school. He probably started regretting it when he found out what a life we registrars lead."

"So he plans to emigrate."

"I don't know about that. He's taking Ann on holiday next week to meet his parents and see how she likes it over there. She went off this afternoon to buy the tickets. The pathology people aren't under pressure like we are. On the whole."

"Thank you, Dr Porter. Just a few questions now about the night of the murder.

"Did you see Bob Jackson?"

"I saw him slinking off home much earlier. No idea what time."

"And Ann Prideaux? She was here with you when we arrived."

"Yes. Harvey Knott let her go. She was here as far as I know except when she went off to see Jackie Fisher. It must have been about eight because I met her as I came out of theatre."

"Why did she call on Miss Fisher?"

"She'd photocopied some stuff for Jackie for an article she was writing. She's very helpful that way."

"I see. Thank you, Dr Porter. That was all most illuminating. I may need to talk to you again."

"Of course. I'll be here."

Charter went in search of Ann Prideaux.

"Dr Prideaux," he said, "I believe you have just bought two tickets for Australia. May I see them?"

She gave him a long, steady look, then opened her bag and took out a folder which she handed to him. He opened it

162

and found therein two return tickets to Melbourne.

"Thank you," he said. "How long do you plan to stay over there?"

"Probably about a month. William's mother and I will look after him. He's totally exhausted and badly needs a rest."

He handed back the folder. "I hope you have an enjoyable time," he said. "And that all goes well for Dr Parchment. Don't suddenly get the idea of leaving before this date, will you?"

"No. Of course not, Superintendent."

"It is, of course, quite possible to take out insurance to cover the loss on return tickets if one doesn't use them."

"We are going to use them."

"Thank you Dr Prideaux."

As he was leaving the room he turned back.

"Dr Prideaux," he said. "Why didn't you tell us that you'd gone to see Miss Fisher that evening and had actually walked down the lane where the murder took place?"

She looked at him calmly. "I forgot," she said. "I simply forgot. The shock of the news about Gurth put everything else quite out of my head. I just popped over there with some notes I'd promised Jackie, that she needed right away. I must have come back only half an hour before it happened. I don't like to think about that."

"Well, I hope you have told us everything this time, Dr Prideaux. Everything. That's how we solve murders. By being comprehensive and checking fact with fact."

"I promise I believe I've told you everything I know. Good night, Mr Charter."

"Good night, Dr Prideaux."

A call came through from DCI Cartwright in London. "I've seen Mr Hay, sir. Got a full statement from him. Saw him in his room at the House of Commons. He was working there with his secretary. Very pretty girl. He wasn't at all pleased. Asked for you. But he has made a statement and he hasn't got a vestige of an alibi. He claims to have been working at home. His wife was out all evening until after midnight and the nanny sleeps on the top floor with the children. She wouldn't know whether he sneaked out. He could have driven down to Stumpington, done the deed and been back home by the time his wife came home. In any case she might lie for him."

"Splendid," said Charter. "And you've got him under obbo?"

"A surveillance squad from the Met. He's not going anywhere without we know about it."

19

Dr Parchment

NINE O'CLOCK was striking as Charter said, "Now we check Dr Parchment's alibi." They got the keys, let themselves into the sports centre and went across the foyer and into one of the row of doors giving on to it. Above the couch and the table covered with bottles of pungent oils was a grille set high in the wall. Both men looked at it and at each other. The sergeant jumped on to a chair to investigate and found that the grille was screwed on to the wall and it wobbled slightly at his touch.

"He could hardly have got out of that small opening," said Charter.

"Oh yes he could," said Cobbold. "I could myself if I were as thin as he is. I'd get this whole thing off the wall in seconds with a decent screwdriver. He could jam the door with a chair back in case Lily came in too soon and get up and out of here as easy as pie. He looks an athlete and he must be good with his hands."

"Where does it lead to?"

The sergeant was pushing his face up against the grille and squinting horribly in an effort to answer the question. Then he got down.

"It's a sort of narrow passage, sir. It definitely goes somewhere. It really does smash his alibi wide open."

"Then he could have been the avenging angel who stopped the professor in his tracks."

The sergeant got down. "I'll go and investigate the passage." They went together and found that the passage led to the kitchens and the outer door into the courtyard through which they had entered the hospital on the first night.

"So we get him down now?" asked the sergeant.

"I think, Sergeant, we do. Now where's Lily? Ah there she is — Lily! When did Dr Parchment last climb out of the aromatherapy room?"

"Only the once," she said, eyeing him fiercely.

"Why?"

"Why else except because I locked him in? I had a lot on me mind that night and the poor boy went clean out of me head. Locked the outside door and went off home and left him sleeping like a baby. Teased the life out of me next day he did."

"So you think he could have got through, the night the professor was killed?"

"No, of course he couldn't. Aren't I telling you? He wouldn't and couldn't've killed the professor. Besides he had visitors that night. She come running down looking for him and they went off together hand in hand. He didn't wait for no tea that night."

"What time was that?"

"Must have been near on nine-thirty because I was just going to brew up me early cuppa."

"Was this the young woman you saw with him?"

He showed her a picture of Sophie.

"That's her, all right."

"Had you ever seen her before?"

"I knew her all right. Never seen

her with him before but she's the photographer lady what took the pictures of everyone in the hospital for the papers. Asked me some silly questions she did an' all."

"Do you know where they went when they left that night?"

"Me ask the doctor where he's going? Give us a chance! I mind me own business I do?"

"Come on, Lily, I'd like to bet you had a very good idea where they were going. You're sharp as a needle, you are."

"Well, there was someone she had to meet in the caff round the corner. Couldn't catch the name."

"And you haven't seen them together since that night?"

"Haven't set eyes on the blonde piece since then. I give you something to think about, haven't I? If you want me again just give us a shout. I'm always down here of an evening."

"Indeed we shall." They shook hands and left.

"Right," said Charter, "get that young man down here."

Dr Parchment came into the murder

control room yawning.

"Dr Parchment," said Charter, "I want you to think carefully before you answer but then I want the truth. Did you see Sophie Saltram on the night the professor was killed?"

"I don't have to think about it at all, Mr Charter. The answer is, yes."

"Enlarge on that," said Charter.

"Well, she turned up in the sports centre."

"At what time?"

"Oh, I suppose about nine."

"And how long had you been in the sports centre by then?"

"I came down about eight."

"Why did she come? It was rather late at night."

"She just popped in for a chat."

"About what?"

He looked at them and a desperate look came into his eyes. Then he dropped his eyes, looked up again, and said, "Oh well, I suppose you'll have to know. She'd lost a letter. Prof had found it and wouldn't give it back. She thought I might have some influence with him."

"What was in the letter?"

"It was an indiscreet letter from Oscar Hay. It could have cost him his ministry. She felt guilty and wanted to stop the Prof. She asked me how we could stop him."

He looked up and a light dawned.

"Oh no," he said, "she didn't do it. And neither did I. You can check the times. He was dead by then."

"Asking you to stop him when she knew he was already dead would be quite a subtle way of creating an alibi."

"Oh no," he said, "Sophie isn't like that. I got to know her quite well these last few weeks. She used to come and chat to me and Lily'd make us tea and leer at us."

Charter and Cobbold exchanged glances. Naughty old Lily had lied to them over that too. Over what else as well?

"So where did you go when you left the sports centre with Sophie Saltram that night?"

"Just as far as her car. I took her to her car."

"How very chivalrous of you."

"It was pub throwing-out time. Even in Stumpington you get some rough

171

customers that time of night. Might be unpleasant for a gently nurtured female as the saying goes."

"That's your estimation of Sophie?"

"No," he said irritably. "I'm just talking off the top of my head. I'm too tired to concentrate. Sophie can look after herself. But I'm gently nurtured enough to want to protect a female from harassment or annoyance or harm."

"You didn't do a very good job, Dr Parchment. Sophie has disappeared."

"Sophie? You must be joking! Why should Sophie disappear?"

It was very well done but Charter judged it a theatrical performance.

"Do you know where she was going when you left her in her car?"

"I watched her drive off. She didn't say, but I assumed she was going home to her children. Has something happened to Sophie?"

"We'd hoped you might have been able to help us to find that out."

"How can I help? She didn't tell me a thing. I honestly don't know where she is. It can't possibly have anything to do with Prof's death."

"Did Sophie mention seeing anyone in Stumpington on her way to see you?"

"No. I expect she did see half the hospital staff but she wouldn't think it worth mentioning. Go into a hospital and you expect to see a few assorted doctors and nurses."

"I was thinking more of someone who had no ordinary business in the hospital or perhaps even in Stumpington. Someone whom she might have been surprised to see in Stumpington."

"Someone from Penchester or from London? Perhaps Oscar Hay? You want me to give you evidence that Oscar Hay was in Stumpington that night? Well I'm afraid I can't. But he might well have been. He's haunted the hospital since his little girl died. It takes some parents that way. He's nearly driven us all crazy."

"Do you think he was right to blame Professor Tancred? Was the professor incompetent? Or was he perhaps drunk?"

"Certainly not incompetent. Drunk? Who's to say? I couldn't possibly stick my neck out on that one."

"Would you have conspired with the rest of the hospital staff to protect

Professor Tancred's reputation and to make it impossible for Hay to sue him?"

"I really don't know what I'd have done. I wouldn't have wanted him to be disgraced but I'd certainly have wanted to stop him."

"From operating?"

"In those circumstances, yes."

"You mean the circumstances of his being drunk?"

"If he was."

"Is there evidence that his operations were going wrong?"

"There has been a higher level of failed operations over the last few years. No one can be sure of the reason. There are too many imponderables. It's difficult to compare like with like. But people have suspected that he sometimes had the drink taken. Never obviously so. He carries it very well. I've suspected something of the sort. But I've absolutely no evidence of it, so I'm not making any allegations."

"And if Hay had decided to sue would you have testified for Tancred?"

He flinched visibly at the question

then looked Charter in the eye and said, "I'm afraid I would. I think I'd have tried to get an internal inquiry and done something about it privately. But public obloquy for Prof, I couldn't wear it. Do you think I haven't thought about how easily I could make a mistake myself? And any mistake I might make could be fatal. We all live with that. The long hours. You get so tired you can hardly see straight. How could any of us point a finger at Prof when you're always thinking 'There but for the grace of God go I'?"

"So in fact you have been torn between two courses of action?"

"In a way, yes."

"You must have been under considerable strain."

"I'm always under considerable strain. A hundred hours a week, remember? If I'd had time to think I expect I'd have found a way to stop him."

"Well he has been stopped now, hasn't he? In spite of the fact that it seems there was no one in this hospital prepared to do his duty by the patients."

Parchment made no reply.

"Did you leave the sports centre at any time before Sophie Saltram's arrival that night?"

"No. I was asleep in there. Ask Lily. She must have told you."

"Have you ever climbed out through the grille on the wall of the aromatherapy room?"

He looked up sharply. "How did you know?"

"My sergeant found that the grille had been loosened; and checked that there is a way out from the passage on the other side. Very convenient for the lane where Professor Tancred's body was found. So I'm afraid, Dr Parchment, that your alibi no longer holds water. You could have climbed out through the grille at any time that evening."

"I did climb out of it one night when Lily locked me in by mistake. Then the grille was put back on again by one of the porters and I haven't used it since. Are you arresting me?"

"No. There are plenty of people in the hospital with both motive and opportunity. Your motive might be this. You suspected he was an incipient

176

alcoholic and went after him and struck him down to save the patients. It would be a crazy act but there could be mitigating factors. But if you did that you need help. Did you do it?"

"I would say I didn't in any case wouldn't I? So that wouldn't get us much farther."

"Go back to bed, Dr Parchment. Oh by the way, I hear you are off to Australia."

"Yes. Ann and I are off there on holiday to visit my parents."

"I hope nothing prevents you from going."

"Thank you." Dr Parchment walked away.

Charter went home to face another restless night. The fear for Sophie was there continuously now. A dull pain round his heart. And sometimes it leaped into his throat and caught at him so he couldn't speak. He noticed that his breathing had become shallow almost as high up as his collar bone. And in his chest and abdomen was an emptiness that made him feel sick with fear for Sophie.

20

Second Breakfast
with the ACC

AT 7.45 the next morning Charter and Godfrey Baldwin were drinking coffee together again, in the Baldwins' kitchen.

"Any progress?" asked the ACC.

"A call went out early yesterday morning for the car. No luck. It's probably hidden away in a garage somewhere.

"DCI Cartwright has been up to London to interrogate Oscar Hay and established that he has no alibi for the evening of the murder. The Met have got him under surveillance.

"Searches of the three houses in the lane and of the hospital and its grounds have not come up with the shoes to fit the print in the lane, or the bloodstained outer clothing worn by the murderer, or with the letter.

"The hospital administrator, Mr Jackson, had damaged his hand by scalding when we went to see him. I examined the hand in case this was a story invented to hide the fact that his hands were bruised by struggling with Tancred. The hand was inflamed but not bruised.

"Silke von Treiben has left the Tancred house and has not yet been in touch with her parents in Hamburg. We can find no sign of her at any of the ports. DCI Cartwright is setting up a full-scale search today.

"Dr Prideaux declares firmly that Tancred was above reproach as a surgeon but she may be shielding Dr Parchment who worked with Tancred. She has declared her love for Parchment and is going to Australia with him to visit his parents. We're keeping an eye on that little trip.

"We've interviewed the cleaning lady at the hospital sports centre and she has given Parchment an alibi which Sergeant Cobbold checked and found wanting. Dr Prideaux has no alibi.

"I've managed to establish (with great difficulty because the hospital staff are being so discreet that they are almost disappearing up their own orifices) that there was a suspicion that Tancred sometimes operated when slightly under the influence. According to one of the registrars there is a patient who will need care for the rest of his life after an operation carried out by Tancred. No one can say that it was Tancred's fault but the result was not expected and Tancred had the drink taken on that day. Or so some of his colleagues feared. The registrar claims that this was not the case with the operation on Hay's child and that in that case Tancred did a brilliant job and was in no way to blame for the little girl's death. It seems that Hay discovered quite recently what had happened to the brain-damaged patient in the side ward, and, having already heard rumours about Tancred's drinking, he got the idea that his child had been killed by a drunken surgeon. If you agree I intend to go up to see Hay this morning to ask him what he has to say about all this. It seems to me that Tancred might have rung Hay and told him he had the letter and planned to use it to destroy his political career unless he promised to leave Sophie alone. Either for Sophie's sake or for Mrs Hay's. And of course he may have wanted to stop Hay from suing, which would have destroyed his career. Have I your permission to go ahead on Hay?"

"Another twenty-four hours, John. Not a minute more. It does look like Hay, I'll grant you that, and you've made progress. But unless you can actually nail him by this time tomorrow we go to the Chief. I don't believe for a moment that he'll take you off the case now that we've got so far, but be very careful, John. You'll have to handle Hay carefully."

"I'll be careful, sir."

"Is the German girl going to be another murder inquiry?"

"Can't say at all, sir. She could have gone off with a lover of either sex. She could be on her way home to Hamburg. She could have seen something in the lane that gave the murderer a fright. He may have felt she must be silenced. And, another possibility is that she dealt the blow herself. She's quite a hefty young woman."

"And no news yet on Sophie?"

"Not yet. I'm leaving DCI Cartwright in charge of the search for the German girl. And while I'm in London I'll see Hay's wife and check his alibi. He seems to have none but if I could find he had in fact an unassailable alibi, he'd be out and we'd be free of a difficult situation."

"Yes. That could be a real headache."

"Special Branch, yes. But I don't think we've put a foot wrong so far, sir. I've checked and he isn't involved in anything remotely sensitive. Discreet surveillance by a Met team can't do any harm as long as the Press don't get hold of it."

The ACC almost appeared to shudder at such a suggestion.

21

The House of Commons

A TELEPHONE call ascertained for Charter that Oscar Hay went early each day to his office at the House of Commons.

He parked his car in Great Peter Street and walked along between the Embankment and the Abbey to St Stephen's entrance. The wind and rain lashed at his face and whipped his coat out behind him as he strode along. By the time he turned in and explained himself to the PC on the door he was cold as well as despondent.

As he walked through the lobby among the Members of Parliament, the lobbyists and the uniformed policemen it seemed a fantastic notion that he could be suspecting the man he was here to meet of murdering two, perhaps three, people. When Hay appeared before him looking perfectly normal and sensible and led him to his office, Charter almost felt that he had allowed his imagination to run away with him.

Charter brought out Sophie's folder and spread the photographs and the notes out on the table in front of Hay.

Hay looked at them and turned to Charter without showing any reaction at all.

"Well?" he said.

Charter said, "We know that Sophie Saltram was working for you on the research for a television programme which was to exposé the malpractice you believed was the cause of your daughter's death."

"And?"

"You said nothing of this in your statement."

He sighed wearily. "Mr Charter, you must know as well as I do that an MP has to be very careful about adverse publicity. Now that the professor is dead so is the idea of the TV programme. The danger is over so I don't have to stop him. He can no longer condemn a patient to death or destruction. It's over."

"Mr Hay, a young woman has

disappeared. We're concerned for her safety."

"I'm sorry to hear that but it's nothing to do with me. Any MP's name in connection with that ingredient is political death."

"Political death can be well deserved. My job is homicide. If you had told us about the exposé Sophie was working on for you you'd have saved us hours of work. We're looking for a man who has killed once and may kill again, and for a woman who is missing in that context. It seems strange that you obstruct our enquiries, particularly in the circumstances."

"Which circumstances?"

"That you had been lovers."

"Lovers? What gave you that idea?"

"The love letters, Mr Hay. And the night you spent with her at Bray."

"Bray? I've never been to Bray in my life. What on earth are you talking about? Your sister must have been fantasizing and I must say I'm disappointed in her. I fell for her (misguidedly, it now seems). She turned me down. End of story."

Now Charter was hiding a smile. Never

been to Bray in his life! Sophie had made it all up! How clever of her! She knew him too well! And where, oh where, was she?

"It amuses you," said Hay coldly, "to hear that your sister invents sexual fantasies about herself and prominent public figures?"

"Oh no, Mr Hay," he said firmly. "It was no fantasy. It was a lie. And Sophie is a very truthful girl. If she told me a lie it was for a very pressing reason and when I know that reason I think I may well be on the way to solving this case."

"You don't seem to have done particularly well so far."

"No. We haven't. And that, Mr Hay, is because everyone in the hospital has been totally obstructive. I think I'm beginning to understand why. I believe you too, sir, are being obstructive."

"You see me as a suspect then?"

"Your visit to me showed that you were very anxious about the letter Professor Tancred had found in the pocket of the anorak. That could have been a motive."

"The letter might conceivably have lost me my seat in the Cabinet, but I would hardly kill to save my political career."

"Perhaps you suspected that medical malpractice was the cause of your daughter's death. Did you plan to sue?"

"I discussed it with the lawyers and decided not to sue. I can refer you to my lawyer if you wish."

"I'd rather hear it from you."

"Very well. But you must be quite clear on one thing; if we'd won we'd have put the money into a fund for other victims of medical negligence. We weren't trying to screw large amounts of money out of the NHS for ourselves. But unfortunately you can't broadcast what you would have done with the money if you've no chance of getting any. I don't like carrying that stigma."

"I doubt if anyone would see it like that, sir."

"Oh yes they bloody well would. You're obviously not familiar with the concept of *schadenfreude*. People like to look upon a successful politician as a shit?"

"When did you take the decision not to sue?"

Hay gave him a hard look then said reluctantly, "I suppose it was about two weeks ago. They persuaded me that my wife was right. She always said don't do it. You can't win against the medical profession unless they decide to let you and this time they certainly won't. It's too public. The child of an MP. Well, she was absolutely right. You've got the lot of them against you — the Secretary of State and the BMA, the General Medical Council, the Medical Defence Union, the Regional and the District Health Authorities and God knows who else. They have access to public funds and we're too rich to get Legal Aid. Only a multimillionaire could afford to take them on without Legal Aid.

"We got a very good lawyer but you can't get a lawyer as good as theirs. Theirs are totally skilled in the subject. They know how to delay you and stop you and circumvent you. Only a fool would try to take them on. I found out what the percentages are. Eighty-six per cent win their cases for compensation in ordinary claims for injury but in cases of medical negligence it's only thirty five per cent. How do you prove that the doctors or nurses fell short of reasonable standards of care? And then you have to prove that it was that failure and no other that caused the injury. You can't get the facts you need. Important documents go missing. They can't find the records. The official you need to rubber-stamp some vital form can't give you an appointment for several months. You can't win against that sort of thing even with the best advice."

"And you can't get them to settle out of court?"

"That's a nightmare situation. If they offer to make a payment into court you might accept it and avoid the possibility of having to pay for an expensive court case for which you'd have to pay all the costs if you lose — including those of your opponents. But if you accept the payment into court you won't be entitled to more than that amount even if you win the case. So, by arranging that you won't be crippled financially if you lose, you make quite sure that you can't win. It's a harrowing decision for anyone without serious money."

"So you threw in the sponge?"

"I threw in the sponge. There was another reason — another of the nightmares — just imagine, Charter, if you had the bad luck to get a judge who was a Mason. Perhaps one who belonged to the same lodge as the defendant. There isn't a jury on medical negligence cases. That judge is the sole arbiter on fact and law. He would clobber you, wouldn't he? And that, Mr Charter, is why I hired your sister to help me research the television programme that was to do the job for me."

"But you didn't explain to Sophie what you were after?"

"No. I just told her to get me all she could about Tancred. All the facts, all the gossip. I told her it was to be the first of a series on prominent figures in various environments. I explained that I wanted both sides of the coin, the bad as well as the good. I needed interesting material to show the TV company to persuade them to do the programme. I thought a clever girl like Sophie might get on to the problem with Tancred herself. If not I could have set the professional researchers on to it."

"I'm afraid she wouldn't be at all pleased at being used like that without a proper explanation of what you were after."

"Well, it's all water under the bridge now. By the way, one of the things that persuaded me to give it up — I began to notice that things were going wrong for me in my career. I lost the chairmanship of an important Commons committee that I'd been told was in the bag. Someone told me about an unpleasant rumour about me that was going the rounds. Lately I've even had the idea that I was being followed. I was blackballed for a club I didn't much want to join, but someone had put me up. Very embarrassing that sort of thing. It upset my wife. I've no idea who it was. But that made me take the decision to give it up. I couldn't put my wife through all that when she was against my doing it from the beginning. And I have to say that since I made that decision there has been a definite thaw in the atmosphere at home. So perhaps I should be grateful to them for stopping me. But I don't like to be bullied, Charter."

"I suppose to get reasonable damages you'd have to go to the High Court and risk being impoverished by the fees."

"Exactly. Our costs, if we lost, would be far greater than the damages we'd have got if we won. They rate the death of a child at three thousand five hundred pounds." Oscar Hay walked to the window and stood looking out for a moment. Then he turned back. "For injury they step it up quite a bit. But in practice that's no help because you can't win. By fair means or foul they make it almost impossible for you to get the evidence you need. After years of the law's delays and the frustration and the expense most people throw in the sponge as we did.

"I hope you find your sister. She strikes me as the sort of girl who might simply go to ground for a while if things got complicated. To think about things and make up her own mind what to do. That's how I read her. Wouldn't you agree?"

"I've no idea how to read her," said Charter. "That's all I need for the present. Thank you, sir."

As they turned, outside the door, to walk away in different directions, Hay shot him an oddly deprecating glance. As he walked off he looked somehow diminished, his chin sunk on his collar, his shoulders slumped forward, no longer the up-and-coming politician. And Charter could find no satisfaction in this.

22

Belgravia — Mary Hay

CHARTER decided to talk to Oscar Hay's wife. The Hays lived in a tall terraced house in Belgravia with a pair of life-sized stone greyhounds flanking the London green-painted door.

Mary Hay came to greet him, shook his hand as if he were a long-awaited guest, and took him into a small study where she offered him a sherry which he politely refused.

She was tall and rather thin with straight dark hair cut to swing below her ears. She had dramatically cleanly-cut eyebrows and a wide mouth which was both sensitive and resolute. Charter was surprised. He had expected a woman suffering both from grief and resentment. This woman seemed calm, friendly and even, in a way, content.

"What can I do for you, Mr Charter?"

she asked. "Do you want to know what I was doing last Tuesday night?"

"Not at the moment, Mrs Hay," he answered. "What I want to know is whether your husband could have gone to Stumpington that night, whether we can eliminate him from our inquiries, or whether there is any chance that his animosity against Professor Tancred could have resulted in what happened."

"There is no possibility," she said, "that Oscar could have committed murder."

"One can picture him acting rashly, perhaps in a rage?"

She said calmly, "I know he comes over on television and in the House as a tiger about to spring but he isn't like that at all. He can rend people verbally, but in real life, physically, he wouldn't say boo to a goose."

Charter looked at her incredulously and she smiled.

"No I promise you it's true. He's terribly squeamish. Can't stand the sight of blood. It makes him sick. When he was a small boy he saw a puppy he'd been given, squashed to a pulp in front of his eyes in a road accident. His mother told me. She said he never referred to it again and he's certainly never mentioned it to me. He tried to cure himself by working at a hospital when he was a young man and he stuck it out for three months but she said it didn't help. He used to come home, she told me, and retch quietly, alone in his room. It was pretty heroic."

"Very heroic," agreed Charter, and she smiled at him.

"I'm glad you haven't instantly taken against him," she said. "People often do. But he's not so bad really. It's the bark. There isn't any bite."

"He seems to have been extremely revengeful over Professor Tancred all the same."

"No, no. You've got that completely wrong. He simply wanted to stop him. Just that."

"And did you share this feeling?"

"No. Not at all. I tried to make him give it up but he wouldn't. It drove us apart. We almost began to hate each other. But Gurth was a good man, Mr Charter. We got to know him and he became a friend." Tears welled

196

up and rolled down her cheeks. She brushed them away impatiently. "He never operates unless there's no other way and he told me how he hates it. When you've finished operating, he said, you just wait for the child to cry. If it cries you know that it's going to be all right. Caroline didn't cry."

Charter had to force himself to concentrate on what she was saying. There was a heavy feeling in his chest, an almost painful constriction that made him aware of how he had depended on the hope that Hay was his man and that Hay would lead him to Sophie without loss of time. It had to be Hay because he was the only one Charter could remotely hope to nail within a few hours, if it proved a true bill. Mary Hay had quietly destroyed every hope he had of catching Tancred's killer by tomorrow's deadline.

Mary Hay paused then went on, "I'll tell you something that may help to establish Oscar's alibi. That night I came home after midnight and Oscar was there and we just went into each other's arms. We slept together for the first time in months. I would have known if he'd just come from killing Gurth Tancred. Do you believe me?"

He looked at her. "Yes," he said reluctantly, "I think I do. You've given him a pretty foolproof alibi."

She took him to the door and bade him goodbye still with as warm a courtesy as if he were a welcome guest. The wives of MPs probably learned that right at the start, and their guests probably learned just as soon not to allow themselves to be influenced by it.

He pulled up his collar against the rain and walked back to his car, hands in pockets, deep in thought.

A foolproof alibi. Yes. But only if Mary Hay was telling the truth. That had to be checked at once and he knew what would be the quickest way to do it. He went to a hardware shop in Pimlico, then took his purchase to the House of Commons and was escorted once again to Oscar Hay's room.

Hay stood up and came to meet him. "What is it? Something new?"

"No, sir. I have one or two more questions to put to you. But first" — he turned away from Hay, took a handkercheif from his pocket and stabbed himself in the thumb with the Swiss army knife he had bought in Pimlico, swung round and showed the spurting blood to Oscar Hay.

The experiment was embarrassingly successful. Oscar Hay drew in a rasping breath and went down like a stone. Charter sent the secretary off to fetch help, wound his handkerchief round the bleeding thumb and checked that Hay was breathing regularly. Within a minute Hay was sitting in his chair being ministered to by a nursing sister who, with the help of various wandering first aiders, presided over the health of the Palace of Westminster.

Charter slipped out of the room. At the door he turned back to Hay.

"Sorry, sir," he said. "Small accident. I shan't need to trouble you again."

He found a first aider and emerged from the House ten minutes later with the deep wound safely disinfected and bandaged. He hoped that Oscar Hay was feeling better. It was not the sort of action he would have taken in any other case. This time the urgency seemed to justify his action, but he knew that it was only because of Sophie that he had done it. If Sophie was in danger no holds were barred.

He went away. Hay was out. This left him deprived of his chief suspect and without another to put in his place.

He went to the Duke of Wellington and ordered a small brandy, drank it very slowly standing at the bar and went on his way.

23

Pinbolt House

A LIGHT mist was coming down over Chelsea and showed every sign of lingering and making his journey home a nightmare but he decided to go over to the City before driving back to Penfoldshire. He went to Pinbolt House and was lucky enough to find Hartley Godwin at home and alone.

"I'm sorry to interrupt you, Hartley," said Charter, as he saw the desk littered with open books and piles of papers and the chair thrust back when Hartley rose to answer the bell.

"I'm glad," said Hartley. "Time for a break."

"Do you think it's me she's hiding from?" asked Charter abruptly.

"How could I tell? She's very fond of you, you know."

"She's an odd way of showing it."

"She worries about you all the same."

"Indeed?"

"She says absolutely no one living alone runs an expensive Aga."

John smiled.

"Of course I know why you have an Aga," and Hartley pointed to his own.

John frowned.

"It's the welcoming hearth in an empty house."

"I see." John looked at him enigmatically, then, "It's not all that expensive," he said. "Did you know that Sophie was working on research for Oscar Hay? He was planning to get some TV company to do a programme for Channel Four on medical negligence with special reference to Professor Tancred."

"Yes, I knew that." Hartley was looking at him warily.

"Have you seen her lately?"

"Not very lately."

"Then how do you know I have an Aga in the new house? You haven't been there and Sophie didn't know I had one until she came to see me that evening."

"She telephoned me."

"When?"

"I can't remember, John."

"Try."

"Let me think. It must have been early on the morning after."

His heart leapt. "You can't imagine how that delights me. Did she sound herself? She wasn't under duress?"

"I hardly think so. She wouldn't have been discussing your domestic arrangements if she were under duress."

"True." He was smiling. "Hartley, may I look in your garage?"

"John, I wish I could help you about the whereabouts of Sophie's car but there is no space in the Pinbolt House garage."

"I see." He stared at Hartley. "I could throttle you, Hartley," he said. "This has nearly killed me. The worry about her."

"She's been safe though, hasn't she?"

"So you kept her safe for me."

"John, you know Sophie. No one could keep her safe unless she had her own reasons for lying low."

"And what could those reasons be?"

"If I knew, John, I doubt if I could tell you."

"You do understand, Hartley, that

from now on this building is under surveillance?"

"No point in that, John." His eyes were amused.

"She's gone?"

"The minute we heard your voice. She went out the back way."

"Why, Hartley, why?"

"I think you'll find she's protecting someone."

"Not Hay?"

"Not Hay. And I can't tell you more than that except that it was Hay who brought her here."

"I see."

"I've kept an eye on her, John, and I've given her good advice."

"And do you know where she's gone?"

"No, I don't. But, knowing Sophie, I'd be worried about her now. I'd find her fast. I know she's worried about the young registrar. She'll be in that hospital and that could be dangerous. Couldn't it?"

"So you positively can't tell me any more?"

"My word once given, you know, John. And now you seem to know all I know."

"I'll go, then. If she phones make her phone me. Don't let her off the line until she says she will."

He drove home through the late afternoon. All the cars had their headlights and fog lights on and the mist came in drifts, thickening and then parting and vanishing, only to gather again a little further on. It had stopped raining but the roads were still wet and as he neared Penchester he could see the low-lying fields in the valley of the River Pen towards Stumpington were covered with a sheet of still, pale water which reflected the oddly truncated shapes of trees and hedges whose tops still showed above the flood.

As soon as he got home he rang Mill House but the phone went on ringing in an empty house. Sophie wasn't there. And if she had been there she would have found the children gone. She'd ring Clarissa. Perhaps she'd even go to Clarissa's to find out where they were. Well, they were safely at Rope Walk and if she wanted to see them she must come to him.

He waited for half an hour at Rope

Walk hoping that Sophie would either ring or appear on his doorstep. Then he knew he must go although he was strangely reluctant to go on with the inquiry. All he wanted to do was to find Sophie and cure himself of this terrible leaden weight that deprived him of energy and purpose.

24

The Coach House

THERE was no more than fourteen hours left to him now before the deadline set by Godfrey Baldwin. Unless he had his murderer by eight o'clock next morning, the ACC would take him off the case and put the whole thing to the Chief Constable who, because an MP was involved, would undoubtedly go to the Commissioner at the Yard. Black marks all round for John Charter. If only he could find Sophie safe and sound none of that would matter to him.

He must put all that out of his mind and concentrate on the practicalities of the case, the first of which was to check with the Incident Room, and whether anything had been learned about the disappearance of Silke von Treiben. By now they must have searched the three houses in the lane and the outbuildings where Myra kept her goats. His mind slid away from this idea, but when they told him at the station that the sergeant was at the Tancred house he went straight there and found him in the coach house. There were no goats there and there was no sign of Myra Tancred. Several officers in overalls were methodically searching the pens.

Cobbold came to meet him, and they walked away across the courtyard. "We can't trace Miss von Treiben through any of the ports and they've heard nothing from her in Hamburg, so DCI Cartwright is setting up a full-scale search for the girl."

"Where is Mrs Tancred?"

"She's out in the field with the goats, sir. We told her we were going to need this place for a while, so she went off in a huff. The water's rising and they expect that field will be under water before the night's out."

"So, nothing," said Charter, glumly.

"Oh no, sir. We've had a big stroke of luck. One of the young constables searching the grounds remembered that one of the trees near the lane where we

208

found the body is hollow. He used to play there when his mum was working in the hospital kitchens. He's a keen lad so he went back and had a look and found what looked like dirty old pieces of string. When he got them out he got quite excited. It's the plastic mac, sir. He cut the seams off. Suppose he thought he couldn't get rid of them as easily as the rest of the mac so he cut them off and chucked them away. Then when young Harrison was walking away he thought again and went back and rummaged about and he came up with two of the buttons. Same beige colour as the plastic. Forensic should be on their way up there soon."

"So who, Derek? It's likely, isn't it, to be one of the three from the houses in the lane? More than three, actually."

"Yes, sir. There's Mrs Tancred and Silke, Miss Fisher and both the Jacksons."

"What would he do with the rest of the mac?"

"We're searching for it, sir. I reckon he cut it up into small pieces. They're going over the three hospital houses in the lane with a fine toothcomb."

Charter thought about the coach house. What about cutting up their mac so small that it would mix with the feed? No. The goats might get sick and Myra would examine it and possibly find the pieces. Anyway it would be almost impossible to get it small enough to mix with the bran or whatever it was she fed her goats.

What about the straw bedding? Cut the thing up as small as you could, scatter it and cover it with a layer of straw and who would ever notice? How often do they clean the floors?

"Sergeant," he said, "get them to find out when the bedding for the goats was last changed and then to search it for minute particles of beige plastic mac which is to go at once to the lab."

"It may be on the muck heap," said the sergeant. "I'll find out. It might even have been spread out on the garden by now." He went off to investigate and Charter thought of the wet floor in the goat house when Myra had taken them into it on the morning after the murder.

Myra had gone over to see whether the tap was dripping and hadn't she made a small tut-tutting sound? So, she thought someone had left the tap on overnight.

It looked as if someone might have washed the plastic mac using the coiled hose at the edge of the milking platform. Then he had sat down and carefully cut up a beige mac into shreds and scattered it over the floor. Did that seem likely?

Who, then?

It could have been Myra. Myra would never have fed a plastic mac to her beloved goats, but scraps of plastic under their hooves could surely do them no harm. And the cutting up and neat disposal of seams and buttons might well be the work of a woman.

What about Miss Fisher? Could she have been a jealous woman rejected by the professor, perhaps after making some declaration of affection? She was clearly aware of Tancred's charm and, like Ann Prideaux, she had been uncharacteristically reduced to tears by the news of his death.

And that brought him to the Jacksons. Could it have been Mrs Jackson? Or perhaps Mr Jackson using Mrs Jackson as an accomplice?

The sergeant came back.

"It's long gone, sir. They muck out every day and it gets carted away. It seems the allotments have all they need at present. They've a huge muck heap out there and they help themselves. A local nursery comes once a week to take the surplus. It went early this morning. I've rung the DCI and he's sending two of the lads over to have a look."

25

Mrs Jackson

WHAT about Mrs Jackson? She had already been interviewed by the murder squad but he decided it was worth while having a word with her himself. After all, Cartwright had interviewed Mary Hay with undoubted professional competence and had learned nothing to the point. A rattle of chains, a scraping of bolts, the turning of more than one key, and Mrs Jackson was peering round the door at them, a look of alarm on her face.

"Well?" she asked with some nervous impatience.

"Detective Chief Superintendent Charter and Detective Sergeant Cobbold," said Charter. "May we come in? I need to ask you a few questions. Nothing alarming."

Without a word she released the chain and stepped back to let them come in.

Mrs Jackson was small and round, with neatly curled hair, a smart suit, a Viyella blouse and pearls. She wore very high heels which brought her up to a height of five feet three inches. She sat down and waved to them to do the same.

"I don't know what more you can possibly want to ask me," she said. "Your men have been practically living here. I can't imagine what they think they're looking for."

"I just want to refresh my memory about the night of Professor Tancred's murder," said Charter. "I believe it was your birthday."

"My birthday? Who said it was my birthday?"

"Wasn't it?"

"No."

"Then why did your husband come home early?"

"He didn't. He often comes home at five-thirty."

"I wonder why your husband told us such a foolish lie."

"Unfortunately my husband lies about all sorts of things. He is so used to telling lies that he hardly knows what the truth

214

is. It's a habit he's got into."

"So you don't think he had any particular reason for telling me it was your birthday?"

"Oh, yes. He had a reason. He wanted to explain that he had to leave his office early. He is rather lazy but he likes people to think that he works himself into the ground. You're looking embarrassed, Sergeant. What's the use of being embarrassed about the truth? I'm telling you this not to put my husband down but because if I don't tell you the truth you might think he had something bad to hide. He lied to you of vanity."

"If that is so Mrs Jackson I wonder how he holds down his job."

"So do I. I always hope but I worry a lot."

"You take a very clear view of your husband, Mrs Jackson."

"I couldn't go on with him any other way. But I'm fond enough of him for that."

"Were you and your husband here together all evening on that night?"

"We were here. Not necessarily together. We had supper together. Then I did

215

some cooking for the freezer, and he went into his study to work. Well, he calls it working. Usually if I go in there he is reading a thriller. So I don't go in. He always pretends he's just picked it up. He knows I know but he has to keep up the pretence. It's very illogical."

"So, do you think he could have gone quietly out of the house without your hearing him, at some time during the evening?"

"No, he couldn't have done that. I would have heard him. I have very good hearing."

"Even with the television on?"

"Even then. But the television wasn't on."

"And you didn't go out yourself?"

"No. I didn't stir out of the kitchen till Jackie Fisher arrived. I called my husband then and we sat here by the fire and Bob got out the brandy. She was in tears. Very shocked."

"I expect you and your husband were shocked too."

"Of course."

"Did your husband get on well with Professor Tancred?"

"Not particularly well. Bob didn't like him much. They argued a lot about hospital business. Nothing serious. I think you could say they were indifferent to each other."

"And you?"

"I'd have liked to get to know him better. He was a very charming man. Nice to women. But we couldn't have him to dinner because his wife hardly ever goes out to parties. He sometimes had a do at home but he always had to get in help until the German girl, Silke, came. She's a sort of au pair. She's rather good at bits and pieces to go with drinks."

"Were you concerned about Myra Tancred when you heard of the murder?"

"Of course we were. We went over to see her but she was lying down upstairs and Silke was looking after her so we sent up a message by Silke that we would do the goats for her."

"And did you?"

"Yes. We'd done it once or twice before. We made it clear that she can't depend on us for that. We don't really want to become regular goat-sitters for her. And, to do her justice, she wouldn't expect it. Besides, she never goes away except for showing and Silke's there if she falls ill. But that night they were both in a pretty ropy state."

"So Myra Tancred is a friend of yours?"

"Certainly not. She's a very eccentric woman. She doesn't play bridge and she doesn't go in for good works. I do a bring-and-buy morning every so often for the NSPCC. She won't come to them. It's not that she's lazy. She just doesn't like human beings. Poor woman. Imagine turning from human beings to goats. And with such a dishy husband too. She's very odd. I wouldn't put it past her to have killed Gurth Tancred herself. I tell you I don't feel very comfortable on my own here any more. I keep all the doors and windows locked."

Her eyes widened and she turned pale.

"I'm frightening myself now," she said. "But what about Silke? They say she's disappeared. First Gurth. Then Silke. Will it be Myra next or has Myra done for them both? There, I've said it." She

218

looked at them, her face horrified.

"Mrs Tancred believes that Silke has left the country."

"Is she back home yet?"

"Not yet."

"Well, then. Have you looked in the coach house where she keeps the goats?"

Charter's flesh began to creep.

"Well," she said, "it's a perfect way out, isn't it? Do you remember that lady — the wife of the newspaperman? On the farm? If I were you I'd look in that coach house. I really would."

There was nothing ghoulish about her urgency. Her eyes were honest and anxious.

"We're doing that," Charter assured her.

"Of course," she said, "it may already be too late. But you know, she showed me those arrangements out there one day, so I'd know what to do. There's the hose and the drainage in the floor — for washing anything away after you've done — the cutting."

Charter got up. He knew Sophie was found but he didn't know where she was, and until he saw her alive and well his imagination still ran riot. The sergeant stepped in as he turned his back on them and walked over to look out of the window.

Cobbold said to Mrs Jackson, "Would you like us to put a guard on the house?"

"No, thank you. A guard wouldn't help. Anyone might get in at the back. You'd need to be all round the house. Now that the girl has disappeared I'm moving in to the White Hart. It's just the other side of the Square. Bob can join me and come home when he wants — to fetch the post or take his telephone calls."

"You're very wise," said Cobbold.

"Well it's the thought of that woman next door really. I keep picturing her creeping in with a knife in her hand. I know it's stupid. She's probably perfectly innocent. But that's the power of imagination isn't it? I never would have thought I was an imaginative person before. But I am and it's awful. It makes you understand why all those geniuses seem to end up mad."

Unwelcoming as she had been, she

now seemed to want to keep them with her.

"If you've got your bags packed," suggested Cobbold kindly, "would you like us to escort you over to the White Hart now?"

"Oh, that is kind of you," she said. "I was waiting for Bob but if you would. He can pack his own things. It doesn't seem to worry him. But I suppose men are different."

They walked over to the White Hart with her and deposited the luggage at the reception desk.

26

Dr Parchment

CHARTER bought the sergeant a beer and himself a small brandy at the bar. Then he said, "The only lead I have is a hint from Hartley Godwin who knows Miss Saltram well. He warned me that she might go to see the surgical registrar at the hospital. I think it was a hint that he's the man she's protecting."

As they walked into the hospital from Market Square they heard the sound of hurrying footsteps and there was Lily wrapped in an ancient fur coat with a scarf over her head.

"Do you know what?" she said. "That night what the blonde lady come down to see my Doctor Parchment they ended up in a muck sweat. They was talking nineteen to the dozen and patting and hugging like they was sorry for their selves. Come to think of it, it was something he says to her that give her a shock."

"Lily," said Charter. "You're a marvel!" And he bent to kiss the withered cheek and walked back into the hospital leaving her smiling like a girl.

Sergeant Cobbold hurried after him.

"Doctor Parchment, sir?" he asked.

"Yes. Dr Parchment," said Charter ominously.

"Is he our man, sir?"

"That remains to be seen but this goes to show that he knows why Sophie ran away. I'll handle this while you check with the station."

Dr Parchment came down looking distinctly wary.

"Have a heart, Mr Charter," he said. "I've got to catch up on my sleep or my patients will know it."

"I know," said Charter. "This won't take long. Now, Dr Parchment, Lily has come clean. She tells me that when Sophie came down to see you that night you told her something that made you both very agitated. Did you tell her that Tancred had been murdered?"

Parchment rolled his eyes heavenwards

223

as if seeking Divine inspiration or intervention. Then he said calmly, "Well, yes, I did."

"How did you know? You told us you didn't climb out through the grille that night and Lily swears you didn't go out through the foyer."

"I didn't go out at all," he said. "I stopped there until Sophie came. But Ann Prideaux came in earlier to tell me the news."

"Oh she did did she? Lily didn't mention that and neither did Dr Prideaux."

"Lily didn't mention it because I told her not to. I told her that you might easily suspect Ann of doing the murder if you knew that she had been in that lane. I wanted Ann to pretend she knew nothing until later."

"Why?"

"Because I thought you would think she had done it."

"Did you think she had?"

"No, of course not. Well, it did cross my mind for a moment. She kept saying 'If only I hadn't left just then' and for a moment I thought she meant 'If only I hadn't left just then I wouldn't have been in the lane at the crucial time and I wouldn't have hit him'. I must have been mad to think Ann could have done such a thing. What she really meant was that if only she had spent half an hour with Jackie Fisher, she might have been going down the lane at the time when he was attacked and she might have stopped the murderer."

"So you believe she didn't do it?"

"Yes."

"And she believes that you didn't?"

"Well, yes. Neither of us could have done such a thing. We were both absolutely fond of the man. I would never have suspected Ann for a moment if I hadn't been at such a low ebb. I'd been on call for too long. I was irrational. Imagine telling old Lily to lie to you! Ann thinks I need a rest."

"So you are off to Australia to take one?"

"That's right."

"Why was Sophie Saltram so upset when you told her about Professor Tancred's death?"

"Surely any girl would have been upset. She thought of him as a good friend."

"She seems to have made a number of good friends in the short time she was conducting her investigations here."

"That's because she's a very interesting and unusual and friendly girl."

"I see. Where did she go that night?"

"Where? I don't know."

"Why did she go?"

"Because I told her I had killed Prof for the sake of the patients. She was shocked but she understood, and she didn't want me to be arrested."

Charter was visited by an urge to hit the young man very hard.

"Why the devil," he said, "did you do that? Didn't you know she would try to protect you?"

"I had to do it for Ann. If I had to, I would have told the police it was me. I know it sounds crazy but I really thought it was Ann and I felt so sorry for her I wanted to take it off her shoulders. I didn't realize the effect it would have on Sophie. She was desperately sorry for us both. And for Gurth. And when I told her I was going to take Ann away to Australia she said she'd go off somewhere until we'd gone so that she couldn't be interviewed by the police and have to give us away."

"We do have extradition arrangements with Australia."

"I know, but it would have given us time. Mind you, I thought at the time it was rather a dotty thing to do. Sophie could simply have lied to the police, but she said she couldn't do that. A very truthful girl, Sophie. Anyway I was in such a state what with being so pooped and I'd taken something to calm me down so I could sleep after the accident victims. Nasty that was. I expect my judgement was a bit haywire. I took her off to meet Oscar Hay. He'd come down to Stumpington for some purpose of his own and she needed to see him. We had coffee together in a cafe."

"You told me outright that you didn't see Oscar Hay in Stumpington that night."

"I withdraw that. He was kind. He's not a bad chap. Bought us both a brandy. Soothed Sophie. Ticked me off for telling her. Told me he would stand by me if it ever came to trial. Then he took her off in his car. She was going to follow him to London to hide her car in his garage and I don't know where she was going after that."

"Right. That'll do for tonight. Come down to the station tomorrow and someone will take down your statement."

"You do believe it wasn't Ann?"

"I believe nothing and nobody at this point in an investigation, Dr Parchment."

27

Consultant and
Administrators

IT was dark now. Charter forced himself to picture himself later that night drinking hot toddy around the Aga with Sophie and the children, but he had no belief in it. His heart felt like lead in his chest. He had a premonition that everything, now that Sophie was found, was going to go wrong.

Eleven more hours. Jackson. Jackson was really the most likely. How much would he have sacrificed to the aim of building up the reputation of St Christopher's? How would the death of Professor Tancred have helped him to accomplish this aim? Would it put an end to the possibility of Hay's suing for damages? Can you sue the dead? Surely not. But you can certainly sue the Health Authority and the hospital. Jackson wouldn't know that Hay had thrown in the sponge and had no intention of suing.

There were other bones of contention between Jackson and Tancred — matters to do with hospital administration. It could be that such matters were crucial to Jackson's ambition and Charter had no doubt at all that Jackson was a very ambitious man. It seemed that Tancred must have been a continual check on this burning ambition. Supposing some vital question to do with hospital administration had come up?

He hesitated for a moment between Harvey Knott and Miss Fisher. Harvey Knott had been a closer associate of Tancred but Miss Fisher was more open and easy to read and much more forthcoming and she must know quite as much as Jackson about hospital business. He decided on Miss Fisher and found her busy in her kitchen.

She took him into the drawing-room then went to turn the oven off and came back smiling and flushed as if she were blushing again. Perhaps she fancied him. In which case he had misinterpreted the circumstances which would cause her to blush. This happened to him from time to time. It used to irritate Sophie enormously when they were married though she tried hard not to show it to the languishing females because she claimed it was John's fault, not theirs. However, he could usually read the signs and he didn't think Miss Fisher was the sort to swoon over a chance-met policeman however kindly or perceptive he might be.

She sat down on the opposite side of the fireplace.

"Can I help?" she asked, looking half eager and half frightened.

"Now, you told us that Mr Jackson and Professor Tancred didn't see eye to eye with each other over questions to do with hospital administration. What sort of questions?"

"Bob Jackson was obsessive about the reputation of St Christopher's. His job depends on this hospital's reputation. If things are seen to be going downhill, Jackson's administration comes in for criticism. He is often very ratty with people whom he thinks are not pulling their weight. He would be quite capable of trying to tick off Gurth Tancred and he would get short shrift from Gurth if he did. I explained to you, Gurth wasn't interested in anyone's reputation, let alone the hospital's. He only cared for the facts and the right and wrong of things, not for what people might think of them. He made his decisions on quite a different system of values."

"Which method do you support, Miss Fisher?"

"It makes no odds to me. Of course I'm an admin person myself these days so I see the problems with Gurth's approach. Patients' satisfaction doesn't figure in the balance sheets, though it will if the new NHS Bill goes through. Bob Jackson thinks success can only be measured by the number of high-tech operations we do and the number of expensive pieces of equipment we manage to amass."

"And Tancred wouldn't wear that?"

"Well, he did high-tech operations himself of course, over at Penchester, but he felt it wasn't always right to go overboard on buying scanners and other astronomically expensive equipment because the running costs of high-tech equipment can be so high that you have to close wards to pay for it. Prof would never have agreed to that."

"And would this lead to real animosity? Surely not."

"My dear man, where have you been the last ten years or so? Not lead to animosity? The NHS is positively riddled with animosity. I bet the Police Force is just the same. They are all at each others' throats half the time."

"So in what way did Mr Jackson differ from the professor on the subject of reorganization and did it really matter?"

"I'm afraid it did. Jackson felt that Gurth wanted to keep us forever among the lower echelons. Bob wanted us to become the flagship for the hospitals of the region. He got more and more angry with Gurth."

"Angry enough to kill him?"

"Oh no, of course not. But perhaps angry enough to hit out at him in a rage and make an unlucky hit."

"What exactly was it that Jackson wanted to do and how was he frustrated by Tancred?"

"Well, he wanted the hospital to become an NHS Trust. All hospitals are going to have to decide whether they want to be directly accountable to their own Health Authority or to become self-governing Trusts reporting only to the DOH."

"How would it suit Jackson's purposes for St Christopher's to become an NHS Trust?"

"Well the Trusts will be much freer to manage their own affairs. That would give Bob Jackson much more scope. You know we administrators can increase our pay by a third in performance-linked payments. And we'd have to amalgamate with Penchester. I wouldn't be surprised if Bob has his eye on the top job there. He'd be doing very nicely, thank you, if he were top administrator for the Trust."

"And what would being a Trust mean in practice?"

"Well, we'd opt out of national pay bargaining. We'd set our own rates of pay and conditions of service. We'd be able to attract much higher calibre staff."

"How would you pay them if the

government aren't putting in more money?"

"We'd be a much bigger unit. There'd be fewer units altogether so once they'd done the top-slicing there'd be more for each unit.

"We'd be able to borrow money from the government if the DOH approve our plans and we'd be able to spend on the buildings as well as staff. Our outpatients is a disgrace. And Bob has very big ideas. He wants to set up a postgraduate medical school so we can be more involved with the university. We'd become a regional unit reporting only to the DOH. Nowadays we have to report to the South Pen Health Authority and they report to the Penfoldshire Regional Health Authority which then reports to the DOH. There'd be much less red tape and, as you know, red tape costs money. We'd amalgamate with Penchester to all intents and purposes. Gurth's neurosurgical department would become the regional neurosurgical unit."

"Would that be a good thing?"

"For the hospital, yes. We'd get new consultants brought in. It wouldn't have been so good for Prof. Could have been a bit threatening for him. You might get young surgeons coming in who would be risk-takers, and possibly real high-fliers. There'd be a lot more competition. Gurth had been the kingpin around here for donkey's years. That might change."

"And what if you got into financial trouble?"

"We shouldn't. But Gurth was worried about that side of it."

"It does sound like a possible recipe for bankruptcy."

"Nonsense! It's the most exciting development in years."

"Then Gurth Tancred was a wrecker?"

"He was nothing of the kind. He was just a little scared of something so new. And he was worried about his patients. He was a bit like a mother hen with its chicks. You see, in the new scheme patients might be referred to hospitals two counties away and more. Not very easy for the families who want to visit."

"And would the professor have had enough clout to put an end to these plans?"

"Well, yes, he might. Let's say that now he's gone it will be a lot easier to turn the hospital into a Trust. He was very influential round here. People listened to him. He was so obviously on the side of the angels."

"But he was wrong on this one?"

"Probably. Who am I to say? I'm afraid the angels don't get much of a look-in in hospital administration. It's very down to earth and bloody hard work. We have to deal with so many things you all take for granted. I think honestly that Bob did resent Gurth because he thought Gurth felt he was the big shot and his work was infinitely more important than ours. But, just think, if the laundry service failed or the kitchens went out of action, and then that recurring nightmare of the cockroaches, and the beastly Press, and the horror stories and you've got the safety precautions and the refuse collection, and the domestics, and the social workers, as well as the finances, and the nursing services and the porters, and then they all go on strike. It's no picnic I can tell you. And you can't imagine the amount of paperwork and the directives we have to read from the DOH."

He was looking at her in horrified commiseration and she began to laugh.

"Don't look so shocked," she said. "It's not as bad as all that. We're pretty well paid. But I can tell you we earn every penny."

28

The Jackson Kitchen

HE left the house, grappling with the thought that he had less than ten hours left to go, and that within a short time most of his suspects would be asleep. Well, they could always be wakened up.

He met Derek Cobbold coming towards him up the lane.

"Sir! It's Miss Saltram! She phoned the station and asked to talk to you."

"Where is she? Did they get anything out of her?"

"No. She hung up as soon as she heard you weren't there."

"I must get to a phone."

At the White Hart he dialled Mill House and got no reply.

He tried Rope Walk and got Cathy.

"Oh, Mr Charter!" she said. "She telephoned! Mrs Charter telephoned! She said she'll be home soon and she asked where you were. I told her you were on a murder case. She says she'll ring again."

He went into the hospital and had Dr Parchment bleeped.

"Have you heard from Sophie Saltram?"

"Yes," he said. "She bleeped me just a few minutes before you did. I told her the truth and she nearly blasted me off the telephone she was so angry. But she's all right. So, that's one of the missing girls safe and sound."

"Where is she?"

"I've no idea. She was in a hurry. She rang off."

"Blast!"

He rejoined Cobbold outside.

"Sir," said Cobbold, "there's another thing. The lads searching the Jackson house found a pair of sneakers stuffed into the back of the bottom compartment of the freezer. They've gone up to the lab and they'll be telling us soon what size of foot."

Charter looked at him, a great flood of excitement and relief welling up in him. "We may well nail him on that alone."

"Right you are, sir." The sergeant went off to record time and place and possible participants in the freezing of a pair of sneakers. As he walked away he looked back and felt the authentic thrill up the spine as he saw Charter pacing up and down, his hands clasped behind his back. Detective Chief Superintendent Charter was coming up into the straight. It wouldn't be long now.

Charter concentrated on Mr and Mrs Jackson.

Jackson had gone home from work at 5.30 on the evening of Tancred's death, and that was not unusual. Why would he decide to go out again? He might have gone out to buy an evening paper, to fetch a book he had forgotten, or to consult a colleague on hospital business. He would have met the professor on his way home and at his most irritating, smelling of drink. An argument, a scuffle, and an unlucky blow.

The murderer could have sustained a blow from Tancred's bruised fist. On Jackson this wouldn't show because he wore a heavy beard. So he might have been walking round for the past few days

241

nursing a nasty bruise under the beard. Having done the deed and grasped the enormity of what he had done he decided to conceal the body. When he saw Silke coming along the lane he must have taken to his heels, and when she went into her screaming turn he knew that someone, the police, would soon be there. So he took off his bloodstained mackintosh. He rushed into Myra's coach house and hosed the mackintosh down. He daren't take it into his house because his wife was there, cooking. He got hold of some scissors. Where? The station was checking on that, and he must find out what they had discovered. Then the murderer cut up the garment into small pieces and scattered it into the litter.

A picture came into his head of Jackson's scalded hand. He had examined it to see if Jackson were trying to conceal the fact that his fist was bruised from hitting Tancred. It was the inside of the index finger and the thumb that were inflamed. It was possible that Jackson's hand hadn't been scalded at all. He could have made up the story to hide the fact that his hand was sore from cutting up the heavy mac, and perhaps the sneakers too.

Jackson could have spent a considerable time over at Myra's coach house that evening while his wife was cooking and thought he was safely reading thrillers in his study. Then he could have walked over to the hollow tree and hidden the seams and buttons in the cavity. And all this with police all around him? Not impossible. It was dark and it was easy to see where the police were and to avoid them, for everywhere policemen were searching there were lights of one kind or another.

What would he do with the shoes? He thought over Mrs Jackson's account of the evening. If she had been in on it with him they could have decided together where to stash the shoes until it was possible to get rid of them somewhere else. He couldn't have thrown them away where they might be found in case they could be recognized as his own. Even if his wife knew nothing there must surely have been opportunity during the evening for him to hide them in the freezer while she was out of the room. But he couldn't have intended to leave them there. Why had he left them there so long? Mrs Jackson was at the White Hart which gave him a clear field, and it would be urgent to get them away before the freezer could be searched. It should have been searched right at the beginning. He must have a word with Cartwright about that.

Supposing Jackson was the man, that might explain the disappearance of Silke. If he saw her coming down the lane and then heard her screaming he must have been terrified in case she'd seen him. And all the time when he was disposing of the blood-stained mac he couldn't have known whether she'd shopped him to the police or not. When no one came to arrest him he must have realized that she hadn't recognized him but he must have been afraid she might remember something that would tell her who he was. He couldn't stand the suspense so he decided to kill her.

He may have made love to her, enticed her into his house, killed her there and hidden the body. So where is it?

He went to the murder control room

at the front of the hospital and found the sergeant there.

"They're searching the allotments now, sir," said Cobbold. "They've got the lights out there and they're looking for the girl's body in the Jackson patch. It seems that Mr Jackson likes his vegetables fresh but he never goes near the allotment himself. His wife runs it with the help of a handyman from the hospital — one of the porters."

"We'd better have him in pronto. Who do the other allotments belong to?"

"Mrs Tancred has the next one along and she grows stuff for her goats there. Silke did most of the work. And the one on the other side belongs to one of the housemen, Dr Porter. Someone keeps hens further along."

"Well, Derek, it's beginning to look more and more like Jackson."

29

The Student Nurse

"SIR," said Cobbold, "this morning I had a word with some of the nurses. I found a young student nurse who claims to know Silke well. Do you want to talk to her?"

"Bring her," Charter said, and Cobbold went off and presently brought in a young woman in a nurse's uniform.

Janie Lumsden was Silke's best friend among the student nurses. She was solidly built with a pale, pretty, plump face.

"Oh, Silke's awful," she said, with a nervous giggle. "She likes everyone to admire her but she's an awful girl really."

"You don't like her?"

"Oh, yes, I like her all right. It's just that she doesn't really care about people. She wouldn't care what happened to you. She's really funny that way."

"She is fond of Mrs Tancred, isn't she?"

"You must be joking."

"What do you mean, joking?"

"She thought Myra Tancred was a silly old cow. She'd talk like that. She likes the goats but she doesn't care a snap of her fingers for the old girl."

"Are you sure?"

"Well, she had a fling with Prof, you know. She wouldn't have done that would she if she was fond of his wife? Mind you, Silke was ready for anything in the way of a bit of fun. I've never met a girl quite like her for that. She doesn't care about anything really except larking about and doing herself a bit of good. Prof was too good for her. He shouldn't have let her — it was letting himself down. Do you see what I mean?"

"Have you any idea where she might have gone?"

"No, I haven't at all. She'd make up her mind and then she'd just go, regardless. She's a very odd girl, you know. You could have a really good time with her. She was always on for a bit of a giggle. But I'd never think of going to her for help if I was in trouble. I would almost anyone else in the hospital but not Silke."

"I see. Did she go in for having a bit of fun with anyone else in the hospital — or in the town for that matter — or anywhere else?"

"She had a boyfriend. She wasn't going out with him but they'd sometimes go to the pictures together. She was really highbrow. She'd go to concerts and museums and art galleries. Sometimes Mrs Tancred took her to London to the National Gallery and other places like that. And she used to make Norman take her too. It wasn't his line really. He left school at sixteen. He works in Stanley's Garage near the Institute. But he's a nice boy. We went out in a foursome once. He's very good-looking. Not that Silke cared about that. You'd sometimes think she chose them on purpose because they were so grotty."

"Did she ever go out with any of the hospital porters?"

"She never told me about it if she did."

"And she never told you she was

planning to leave the Tancreds?"

"No. She never said anything like that. She did say one of the high-ups in the hospital seemed to fancy her, but not Prof. It was after that was over. She never said who it was and I took no notice. She was always saying people fancied her or made passes at her. I got very bored with it in the end. I always think you don't need to boast about it if people really do fancy you a lot. Mind you, Silke is different. Sort of foreign. Well she is foreign. She speaks very good English though. Funny English, but you can always understand what she's saying and she never asks you what you mean. She's very clever. She goes to classes at the college."

"Well, thank you, Miss Lumsden. Now can you tell me anything about the nursing system in the hospital? Miss Fisher is the chief nurse, is she? Do you like her?"

"Yes, she's lovely. Everybody likes her. But we don't see much of her. She isn't involved with the day-to-day nursing."

"Tell me about her."

"Well, you wouldn't dare cheek her. If she ever asked you to do anything you'd jump to it. But she always puts it very nicely. We hardly ever see her on the wards. Some of the ward sisters get a bit cross about it, because they think it's part of her job to visit the wards and see patients. But Sister Rutherford always says she'd rather be left alone to get on with it. She thinks it's so long since Miss Fisher was on the wards that her nursing practice is definitely rusty. Imagine that! But I expect it's true. She's too busy managing things and telling people what to do. But one thing — she always sticks up for us. She's very keen for us to get recognition for what we do. She says the nurses are the backbone of the NHS. Well, they'd look pretty silly without us, wouldn't they? She lectures to us sometimes and she always tells us to stand up for our rights. I know she gets very ratty with the administrator and she thinks the consultants need taking down a peg or two. Well, they are a bit uppity. Think they're God, she says. But you know, the Senior Nursing Officer is God as far as we're concerned."

"I suppose the reorganization of the NHS is very much her pigeon?"

"Oh yes. It's right up her street. I get the feeling that St Christopher's is everything to her. She isn't married and I don't think she even has a boyfriend. I can't think why. She's very pretty. Don't you think so? I think she probably works too hard. It's a real shame."

"I see," and Charter was in fact beginning to see — a crack widening into a great ravine in his case against the hospital administrator. Couldn't Miss Fisher fit the bill every bit as well as Jackson? She was in Jackson's house soon after the murder. She brought them the news and that sent them over to look after Myra Tancred. Was she left alone in the Jackson house? Then she could have hidden the shoes which would explain why they were left in the freezer. If anyone outside the Jackson household had hidden the shoes there there would be much less urgency about removing them. It would be hard to believe that the Jacksons would have left them there to be found by the police. But an outsider might have found it difficult to get access to the house again.

He thanked the girl and asked her to wait outside for Sergeant Cobbold.

30

Mr Harvey Knott's Theory

COBBOLD came back into the room.

"A telephone call for you, sir. Mr Harvey Knott. He wants to see you. It's urgent."

"Send him in. But first, Derek, I want you to find out where Norman lives. The boyfriend who works at Stanley's Garage. See if you can get the name and address from Nurse Lumsden. She's waiting for you outside. Go over and talk to him. He may know what happened to Silke. She may even be there with him."

"And one more thing, sir. They've had to postpone the search out there. The flood waters are rising and the allotments are under water. They've dismantled the lights and they'll probably be able to resume tomorrow. The rain's stopped and the forecast's good."

"Thank you, Sergeant."

The pathologist came in looking pale and harassed. There was no cream on his hair today and it looked distinctly tousled.

"Mr Charter," he said, "I've thought about this a long time and I've thought it best to come and see you. I'm very worried. Very worried indeed. I've learned from colleagues who've been interviewed by you the way your inquiry is tending and I would like to give you what help I can. To prevent a mistake."

Charter waved him to a seat.

Harvey Knott leaned forward anxiously. "I'm very worried about Myra," he said. "I've been in to see her. She'd been out in the field with her goats for hours and she was sitting there exhausted and blue with cold. I've known them for years. There's no chance at all that Myra killed her husband. It's been a shock to her and she was an unhappy woman to start with. She's very disturbed at the moment but she will recover. My wife and I will look after her. But you must look elsewhere for your murderer."

"Thank you, sir. But she isn't by any means our only suspect."

"I'm glad to hear it. There have undoubtedly been tensions between colleagues."

"Do you believe the professor was killed by a colleague?"

"I can't say anything about that. I can only tell you what I know about the stresses and strains. I don't know who killed him. I only know it wasn't that poor woman. She and Gurth had grown apart but neither would willingly have hurt the other. I hope nothing I said to you earlier has given you to think otherwise."

"Please go on, sir."

"She won't leave the house to come to us. But I'm in touch with her medical man and we're prescribing tranquillizers. She doesn't go in for medication as a general rule but she is distraught — hands shaking so she could hardly hold a cup. My wife got her to bed and she's had a heavy dose of medication. If you had to interview her I would advise you to wait a day or two. I'll look in on her again tonight.

"She won't be making much sense after the pills she's taken. I thought it necessary to warn you in case you thought this is her normal frame of mind. Before Gurth's murder she was a perfectly competent woman — neurotic but quite well able to cope with the demands of daily life."

"Thank you, sir. I hope we won't need to trouble her. Is there anything more?"

"Well," said Harvey Knott, "you might well get a mistaken idea about Bob Jackson. There was a move in the hospital to get rid of him. Nobody really liked the man. He is a pushy individual and it isn't easy to avoid him. Bad luck for his wife who seems rather a nice woman. Jackson was all for pushing the hospital into new modern techniques, buying scanners and so on. Gurth thought Jackson was a PR man who didn't care a hoot for patient welfare. In that discussion Tancred won all along the line, partly because the wind is changing. And, of course, he was the great man around here and we'd all been used to following in his wake for many years already.

"It didn't matter what new plan Jackson put forward Gurth seemed to succeed in putting a stop to it. Now that was very serious for Jackson. There are very important issues at stake. There would have been a confrontation in the end. No escaping it."

"So you think it was Jackson."

"No. I think nothing of the kind. Jackson could have gone elsewhere. I simply wanted to show that there are alternatives which are much more likely than poor Myra. Jackson is hardly what I'd call an honourable man and he has the manners of an ox but I do not think he would do murder. If I were asked who is the most likely person to have lost her head I would look at Miss Fisher."

"Tell me about it," said Charter.

"The woman," said Harvey Knott, "is nothing but a pest as far as her male colleagues are concerned. She is a competent senior nursing officer. There's no getting away from that. But she has gone in for what they call Women's Lib. It has turned her head. What small wit she once possessed has vanished away. And she is quite insane about the Masons too. She pretends she disapproves of the whole ethos of the thing but the truth of the matter is that she is angry at being excluded from yet another all-male institution. If they decided to admit women she'd soon be more a Mason than the Masons. No balance. A thoroughly neurotic woman. She almost accused me of killing Gurth Tancred."

"And did you, sir?"

Harvey Knot almost gagged, he was so incensed by this question.

"Of course I didn't," he said at last. "What motive could I possibly have had for murdering my colleague?"

"Perhaps you felt he was likely to bring the hospital into disrepute by continuing to operate while he was in a state of incipient alcoholism."

"Nonsense. It was never as bad as that. And, even if that were true, I wouldn't achieve anything by murdering the man. I'd get him treated. I'd consult his minister and his medical man and any colleagues who could help. I'd get it all tied up within the week. He'd be on leave in a luxurious clinic in Switzerland."

"He wouldn't have agreed to go."

"Oh yes he would, if he'd been given the choice between that and the sack. It was gross misconduct if you are right."

"At last, a member of the hospital staff admits it," said Charter. "A lot of tragedy would have been averted if you had put that plan into action long ago."

"I regret it," said Harvey Knott. "It was tragically remiss of me. It was weak and idle. I hesitated to inflict pain on a colleague. I must live with the consequences of that."

Charter almost hugged him, overcome with admiration for so pompous a man who could make so unpharisaical a turn around and admit that he might have been wrong.

"But there is another possibility and I think it is my duty to draw your attention to it. Dr Parchment, Gurth's senior registrar, is in a decidedly nervous state. He is obviously taking too much medication. Some of these young men unfortunately do. They can't sleep so they take a pill. Then they feel groggy when they wake up so they take another to pep themselves up. Now I happen to know that he has been very distressed and worried about Gurth Tancred. Quite recently one of the housemen came and told me he had heard William Parchment talking in a very indiscreet way about Gurth. It was on the subject of a patient whose operation was unsuccessful and a little girl who died. William said Prof ought to be throttled. It was a tragic situation. Gurth was brilliant and was still saving lives. And William was almost like a son to him. They used to foregather in the snug in the bar at the White Hart where they could be private to discuss cases. It must have caused the young man great distress to know that this man he held in such high esteem was letting his patients down by occasional over-indulgence in drink.

"The girl, Ann Prideaux, one of my colleagues, is now his girlfriend. She, too, has been in a nervy condition. It's not much more than three months since her affair with Gurth broke up. Myra's neurotic condition was most unfortunate. It drove her husband to other women. Ann was in an acutely depressed state for several weeks. Then she took up with William and everyone was relieved. But she hasn't seemed happy. I think she worried about William's state of mind. He may well have resented the man who caused her such unhappiness. One hesitates to point a finger at a colleague but I would certainly think seriously about that young man. If he did strike that blow he is in need of treatment. And he certainly ought not to be in contact with patients until he is thoroughly rested and recovered, whatever the truth of the matter."

"Thank you, sir. We'll look into it," he said. "We'll go round and talk to Miss Fisher first. But I don't quite understand what reason you think she could have had for killing the professor."

"They disagreed fundamentally on the future of this hospital. Gurth didn't argue but he wouldn't let them do anything of which he disapproved. He had a great deal of influence. She's an ambitious woman. She and Jackson had great plans. Gurth stood in the way. I have noticed symptoms of hysteria in the woman on several occasions. They wield far too much power in today's world. Things were better ordered when they knew their place. Do you know that nowadays a mere ward sister can be solely responsible for a budget of a quarter of a million pounds? Someone like Miss Fisher has even more power. It turns their heads. I shall say no more. I've given you a hint. I may be wrong about Miss Fisher but it isn't Jackson."

Charter went through the hospital once more and up the lane to Miss Fisher's house and there he found Miss Fisher in tears.

"Come in," she said. "This is getting me down. It's getting everyone in the hospital down. I do wish you could arrest someone and get it over and done with."

This time there was no offer of a drink or even of a seat. They stood facing each other in the drawing-room and Charter said, "We have made some progress, Miss Fisher, and what I would like to ask you is this — were you alone in the Jacksons' kitchen at any time on the night of the murder?"

A look of unbearable irritation came over Miss Fisher's face. "Of course I wasn't," she said. "When they left to go over to Myra's I came here. Why would I go into Molly Jackson's kitchen? And what would it matter if I did?"

"Just a matter concerning alibis," explained Charter soothingly.

"Well, I'm getting thoroughly fed up with being questioned," she said angrily. "What do you think we are? We've got a hospital to run, you know. I simply haven't got time for all this."

"Miss Fisher," said Charter, "who told you Gurth Tancred was dead? You went over to tell the Jacksons. Who told you?"

She stared at him. "What do you mean, who told me? I told all that to your sergeant when you first came to see me."

"I would like to hear it again from you, Miss Fisher."

Miss Fisher suddenly went bright red in the face.

"How dare you suggest that I could have had anything to do with Gurth Tancred's death? If I'd known that you were thinking that I — that I — that it was me — I'd have told you nothing. Do you hear me? Nothing!"

Charter tried to speak but she swept on.

"Why should you think it was me,

I'd like to know? Haven't you talked to the men? I'll be the one they'll throw to the wolves. I'll tell you what, Superintendent Charter, who do you think keeps this hospital going? Who? Well I'll tell you. The Senior Nursing Officer keeps it going. Without me the whole thing would fall apart. Do you know who are the most important people in this hospital? Well I'll tell you. The nurses. It's the nurses who look after the patients, not the doctors or the consultants. Who do you think found out that Gurth Tancred was exceeding my nursing budget by thousands of pounds? Not Bob Jackson. Me. Think what he would have cost the NHS if I hadn't put a stop to it. And then he started getting drunk and botching his ops. How could a man of his stature do such a thing? Because he let himself get so soft that he couldn't get through the day without a drink or two drinks or six drinks! You work and you slave and you get things running smoothly and then what happens? His hand shakes and he botches the job and it ends with an important man like Oscar Hay suing the Health Authority, and everything we've done goes for nothing! He may operate at Penchester but they're our patients. St Christopher's is known as the place where patients get brain damaged through medical negligence. Negligence! I've another word for it!

"No, don't interrupt me. You can just listen to it all now and then leave me in peace. And what about the Masons? They think they're the cream of the county. He was a top Mason in Penchester. Poor Myra! I know how she felt. Why shouldn't we become Masons and have a say in what goes on? All the men get to be Masons and by the time we have a hospital meeting to make an important decision about hospital affairs (which are my province), they've talked it all over between them and decided what they're going to do. Of course they pay lip service and pretend to have a real discussion but it doesn't fool me.

"Gurth Tancred and Alfred Harvey Knott made all the decisions between them over my head and often over Bob's head. Of course we fought it but we didn't always win and it made our life much more difficult. They were even trying to kill the plan for turning the two hospitals into a Trust, the most exciting thing that's happened in medicine for years. And as for all the women! Those young girls were just laughing at him. Myra was quite happy with that rotten little German lesbian. He should have looked for a wife who understood him and was interested in what he was doing and perhaps could even make a contribution."

Then suddenly she stopped and the flush died down and she stared at Charter and then looked away awkwardly, aware that she had said too much.

"Right," said Charter, "thank you, Miss Fisher. Just one thing more. Who told you the professor was dead?"

"No one told me. I went out to get a breath of air and I saw the lights and walked over and talked to someone there. I think he was a plainclothes man."

"Thank you, Miss Fisher. One last question. I believe Dr Prideaux came to bring you some notes on the evening of the murder. Why didn't you tell me that?"

"Because she just put them through

the letter box. I'd no idea when she came. It simply didn't enter my head to mention it."

Within seconds they were in the lane again on the way to the White Hart.

"Is she the one, sir?" asked Cobbold, greatly daring. "She sounds very anti the professor."

"That's what we're going to talk to Mrs Jackson about," said Charter.

31

The White Hart

THEY found Molly Jackson despondently drinking gin and tonic alone in the bar at the White Hart with a police constable standing awkwardly by the door.

"Good evening, Mrs Jackson," Charter said. "I'm sorry to trouble you again. A few more questions I'm afraid. Shall we sit here in a corner or would you prefer to be more private?"

"Oh here," she said indifferently. "Anywhere. I'm beyond minding."

"Mrs Jackson, has it ever occurred to you that your husband might have committed murder?"

"I've told you. He couldn't have done it."

"How can you be sure?"

"I've already told you. He was in his study. He didn't go out."

"I see. What about Miss Fisher? Did

she stay in your house when you went over to Myra Tancred?"

"What has that got to do with it? Of course she didn't stay. Why should she? She went back home."

"Wouldn't it have been more natural for her to come with you to help Mrs Tancred? She is a nurse. She might have been able to help her."

"She and Myra loathed each other. They'd always been at daggers drawn. Jackie rather fancied Gurth and she hated to be with Myra because she was jealous of her. At the hospital she had Gurth all to herself and she'd have liked to have him at home too."

"Mrs Jackson, I'm going to explain to you why we need to know who could have gone into your kitchen that evening. We've found a pair of shoes the murderer was wearing when he killed Gurth Tancred. He knew he had probably left prints on the wet lane so he had to get rid of the shoes quickly. Did your husband bring them into the kitchen and ask you to hide them in the freezer?"

"In my freezer! You've found shoes in my freezer!" She looked dismayed and even frightened and she fell silent for a minute or two.

Charter waited patiently.

Then she said, "Not Bob. I see that you would think it must be him or me or both of us but it isn't. Jackie Fisher has a key. She could have come back. She knew exactly how long it would take us to put the goats to bed. But it could have been William Parchment."

"Was William Parchment here that night?"

"Yes. He came over late that night to borrow a book."

"And your husband was over at the hospital by then?"

"Yes. He didn't come home till much later."

"What time did you put the dishes in the freezer?"

"Not till Bob came home. I forgot about them after the shock of Gurth's death."

"What time did Parchment come?"

"Soon after eleven."

"And was he in the kitchen on his own?"

"Not that I know of. But he was

alone outside the house for ten minutes. I suppose he could have gone in. I didn't lock the door."

"Where did you go?"

"He needed a book of Bob's for a colleague. It was very urgent and the policeman let him through. It was a book that Gurth had borrowed from Bob.

"It was Bob's copy of Speller. Speller Six, they call it. It's the book they all use to look up the law relating to hospitals. They've had some trouble with parents wanting to sue. He needed it for that. They'd planned a conference the following morning. He had to look it up that night and he knew that Gurth had Bob's copy. Gurth had promised to get it out for him. He felt he couldn't intrude on Myra in the circumstances so he asked if I thought I could possibly get it for him. So I did. Myra's quite a tough old bird really. And, in fact, Silke was up and she found it for me."

"Where was William Parchment when you came back?"

"Waiting for me outside my front door. I thought it rather odd that he didn't come with me to the Tancreds."

"What was he wearing?"

"An overcoat."

"Was that usual?"

"No. Now I come to think of it, it wasn't at all usual. He usually dashes about in his white coat without even a jacket."

"So he could have had something hidden in the pockets?"

"Yes, he could. I suppose you mean the shoes."

He stood up. "Thank you, Mrs Jackson. You've been a great help." He went out and found that the clouds had vanished away and a full moon was pouring its cold clear light over Market Square.

He went to the call box and called Rope Walk again but Sophie had neither arrived there nor telephoned. Then he tried William Parchment's bleep number. There was no reply and alarm signals began to sound in his brain.

He rang the station. They had been trying to locate him with the news that Oscar Hay had eluded his followers and no one knew where he was. Was this anything to do with Sophie? Sophie leaves

272

her hiding place with Hartley Godwin and immediately Oscar Hay goes missing.

Speculation was useless. Not enough data. The only thing to do was to find the murderer and thus make sure that Sophie could not get herself involved with him.

His eye fell on a dark-green MG parked in the centre of the Square. He walked over and looked at it. It was the Turbo. Inside was a shooting stick, an Atlas of the British Isles and a copy of the House Magazine. Oscar Hay had indeed brought Sophie down from London and the chances were that they were both somewhere in the hospital now.

Was William with them and is that why he didn't answer the bleep?

It wasn't Hay. He was quite certain of that. The faint in the House of Commons had been genuine. If it was William, and he was coming to feel that it was likely, Hay would look after Sophie. And surely William would in any case be unlikely to do her harm even if he knew that she knew the truth. There was no need for the feeling of utter helplessness and foreboding that took him by the throat. Sophie was no fool and it looked as if she had provided herself with a stalwart bodyguard in Oscar Hay. But he was always pessimistic. He had known too many cases where the worst had happened through some unlucky accident regretted afterwards even by the agent who had caused it. He wanted no friend, even, to be involved in such events, let alone Sophie.

He went into the hospital and learned at once why William Parchment was not answering his bleep. William was hurrying from the basement stairs towards the door.

"Dr Parchment," he called. "Where is Sophie?"

"Can't stop," said William. "Come with me. I've been called into theatre. Emergency going over to Penchester."

They ran to the car park and William said, "Sophie arrived a few minutes ago with Oscar Hay and they wanted to know where they could find you and they also wanted to know why I had told them I killed Gurth Tancred, and who had done it if I hadn't. Of course I couldn't help them but what I did tell them was this and I'm sorry but it sent Sophie flying off the handle again. I couldn't do anything to stop her. I've got this emergency. Go over to Myra Tancred's house. I told them you might be there. You'll find them looking for you."

"Why there?"

"She'd been trying to get in touch with you. I knew you'd talked to Miss Fisher. I thought you might round the evening off by having a word with Myra. And that's what worried Sophie because she thinks it was Myra who murdered Gurth Tancred."

"Why on earth should she suddenly get that idea into her head? What did you tell her this time and was it true?"

"Well, I did tell her something Ann had told me. She didn't mention it before because she'd completely forgotten it. When she got the news of Gurth's death she couldn't think of anything else and then she was so convinced that I'd done it that she didn't even think seriously about other possibilities. You remember, she even forgot to tell you she'd been in the lane that evening. She was in a right state. That's why she's only just remembered that, as she walked back down the lane after giving Jackie the notes she'd brought over for her, Myra was standing at the side of the lane under that tree. As soon as Ann told me that, it was so obvious. Of course it was Myra. She was waiting for him. She always did strike me as a pretty dotty lady and she's as strong as a horse. I've seen her wrestling with that billy goat when he's obstreperous. She must have the muscles of an ox."

"It didn't take all that much strength. The lab has established that he had one of those fragile skulls. It could have been a relatively feeble blow."

William looked at him, completely taken aback. Then he recovered himself and went on, "Well, whatever. I think Sophie's sure she's mad too. When she heard you'd gone to talk to Myra she just said, 'She'll kill him', and rushed off, with Hay after her. I called out to them to wait until they were sure you were there. They aren't trained to cope with that sort of thing — mad ladies lying in wait in secluded lanes."

"She won't answer the door," said Charter. "She's deeply sedated."

"No, she's not. The reason Ann remembered it and came to tell me about it was that she saw her outside her house a few minutes ago in a dressing-gown with a knife in her hand, looking completely mad. I'm really very sorry but I've got to go now."

32

The Flood

CHARTER turned and ran across the courtyard and along the lane that seemed as bright as day with the white stone of the Tancred house almost luminous behind the tall trees in the moonlight. The strong black shadows of the trees stretched out across the parkland.

He found the door ajar and ran lightly into the hall. Oscar Hay said "Sophie?" and came out of the drawing-room and looked at him in surprise. "Where's Sophie?" he asked.

"I haven't seen her. I thought she was with you."

"I told her to wait outside. I wanted to take a look before letting her come in. The door was wide open and that seemed ominous."

Without a word, Charter ran for the door and was down the steps and round the house to the courtyard in seconds, followed by Oscar Hay, who had a good turn of speed but whose reactions were not as fast.

"Myra Tancred's drugged," he told Hay over his shoulder. "She doesn't know what she's doing."

As they ran into the courtyard a barn owl shot out of the coach house gable, spread its wings and soared off, white as the moon. The door of the dairy was wide open and, as they came round the corner, the big double doors of the coach house burst open and all the golden-haired goats came pouring out, their eyes and horns glistening in the moonlight.

Sophie appeared behind them brandishing a broom with which she was driving them on. As Charter and Hay came into sight, the goats veered away from the courtyard and swung towards the path that led to the field where they had their grazing. The goats began to run, emitting anxious bleats.

Behind Sophie appeared Myra in a nightdress, dressing-gown and wellington boots. She ran at Sophie holding a knife in her hand and she was shrieking, "Leave them alone! Leave them alone!"

Sophie gave a little terrified scream and threw the broom at her. Then she was sprinting headlong after the goats with Myra, who had ducked away from the broom, in pursuit, screaming at the top of her voice, "Bring them back!"

Charter ran after them and he could hear Oscar Hay pounding along behind him. Ahead of them, where the field had been, was the pale sheen of flood water under a sky bleached white by the moon. The herd of goats paused and looked back, but Sophie was behind them and the only way onwards was through the half-open gate and into the field. They dashed on and, one by one, plunged into the water, looking like something out of Greek mythology as they drifted out on the water, paddling with their forehoofs followed by Sophie like a goatherd in her skimpy brown jersey and jeans with her curly cropped head. She waded into the water.

"Sophie!" he bellowed. "Swim for it! She's just behind you!"

Myra was shrieking, "Come back! Let

them come to me!" Then she was wading out into the flood, her white nightdress and green dressing-gown floating around her on the water like the petals and leaves of a water lily.

Sophie turned her head and gave another little scream as she saw how close Myra was, and went into a fast crawl which terrified the goats and sent them plunging in all directions, paddling frantically, their heads held up high above the water, their necks arched.

John forged his way into the ice-cold water and Hay went past him in a long shallow racing dive which took him right up to Myra. As he came out of the water beside her she jabbed at him with the knife. Her attention was still fixed on Sophie and the goats and the attack on Hay was nothing more to her than an irritated brushing-off of an annoying interruption to the purpose which held her whole attention — saving her goats from death by pneumonia or drowning.

Hay fell back into the water with a splash and Myra turned away and went into a dignified breast stroke. Charter caught up with Hay who was emerging from the water with a great deal of splashing and thrashing about. "Get Sophie!" Hay said. "This is nothing."

Charter swam after Myra and saw to his dismay that Sophie was, unaccountably, swimming back towards them, her arm round the neck of one of the goats. She was calling out to Myra, "I'll bring them back! Don't worry!"

But Myra was too distraught to listen and she launched herself at Sophie. There was a scuffle, then Sophie had disappeared. Myra was turning round and round, looking for her. Charter got to Myra and wrested the knife out of her hand as Hay waded towards them through the breast-high water. As they all met, a golden head shot up beside them and Charter breathed again. Sophie had dived away from Myra's knife and done her famous underwater disappearing trick which always had the children falling about with laughter. Oscar Hay put an arm round her and steadied her on her feet. She was shivering and sobbing, breathless and gasping. Charter saw that her left arm was bleeding freely and he took her hand and raised it high above her head. He took the knife, ripped a great piece of his shirt and wrapped it round the wound, tying it as neatly as he could with Myra having mild hysterics beside him. "There, Sophie," he said gently, "you'll be fine. Hay, take her. Call an ambulance. Keep it above her head to stop the bleeding. Go on. Are you all right, Sophie?"

"Yes," she said. "I'm fine now." Hay led Sophie away through the flood and Charter turned to Myra, took one of her hands and put his arm round her shoulders.

"No," she said, her teeth chattering.

"Come along," he said. "We'll get you to the hospital. You are too cold. You need to be looked after. They'll get you warm and look after you."

"They'll die," she said, in an exhausted whisper that was as distraught as a scream. "My goats. It's too cold. And they'll get on to the road."

"No, they won't," he said. "I'll phone the vet. You must come with me to give me the vet's name. We'll get him to come with his helpers and round the goats up and check them all and look after them."

"Not the porters," she said.

"No. The vet and his people. They'll be well looked after."

Then she agreed to walk with him to the house. It was a difficult job to guide her along and he was supporting most of her weight. When they got to the house Sophie was lying on a sofa her bandaged arm held aloft by Hay whose own arm was now roughly bandaged. He looked very pale.

Sophie sat up. "I'm going home now," she said.

"You are not," said Charter. "For once you are going to do as you are told. That's a deep cut and it needs attention and you've had a shock and you've practically got hypothermia."

"Then so have you."

"I've not been ducked and chased and stabbed," said John. "I'll get myself looked after too if it's necessary. You and Mrs Tancred and Mr Hay are all going to casualty. I expect they'll keep you in overnight. I wish I could come too but I've a lot to do."

"I notice, sir," he then said quietly to Hay, "that you didn't faint."

Hay smiled. "It was moonlight," he pointed out. "I couldn't see the colour. It makes a difference. Are you arresting her?"

"What for?"

"Well, murder. Isn't she the one? I mean, with the knife?"

"No, she isn't."

"How do you make that out? Surely there can't be two homicidal maniacs about?"

"She isn't homicidal or a maniac. She has simply been very heavily dosed with drugs. To her we must have seemed like horrible monsters out to get her beloved goats. This has nothing to do with the murder."

"Really?"

"You can see she doesn't know what she's doing. She ought to be in bed. Harvey Knott should never have given her such a heavy dose without making sure there was someone to look after her. She obviously worried about the goats and went out to feed them taking the knife for cutting up the food, or for cutting their toenails, for all I know, and when you ran away, Sophie, and, presumably, took refuge in the dairy and then, when she came in, ran on into the coach house, she must have thought you were out to do her goats an injury. It was unfortunate that she had the knife with her."

"It was the knife. I was terrified. I thought if I let the goats out and drove them away she'd go after them and forget about me. But I didn't know they'd turn into that narrow path and end up in the flood. I was horrified. They might have drowned. I hope they are all right."

He went to the phone then and did what he could to arrange that they would be.

All John wanted now was to take Sophie in his arms and thank God that she was safe. But he couldn't. And it was Oscar Hay who led her out to the ambulance.

Myra Tancred clung to his arm and insisted that he should go with her into casualty.

Later the sister sent for him. "Just a few minutes," she said. "I do think it seems important. She's desperate to talk to you. And she's making much more sense now."

He tiptoed into the side ward and Myra sat up and leaned forward.

"Thank you for coming," she said. "You've been very kind. I'll tell you something. That night, Ann Prideaux was waiting for my husband in the lane."

He gave her a long, hard look. "Why didn't you tell us that before?"

"It didn't seem important. I don't really care who did it. I shall be alone now for the rest of my life but no one can do anything about that. I looked out of the window and saw her. I knew she wanted to make him pull himself together. She waited there and when he came he probably shook her off and told her not to be silly. And I expect she hit him with that post that's been lying there. I don't suppose she meant to do it. But he could drive you mad. He drove the poor girl to it. He didn't really understand people. He loved them but he didn't understand them. He meant to be kind. But he was too keen on what he was doing to really

287

get involved with people."

Charter went up to the private wing where Hay and Sophie were. He went in to see her and was allowed two minutes. She smiled up at him weakly.

"What have you done to your hand?" she asked.

"It's nothing."

"You never tied that bandage yourself. It can't have been nothing."

"Don't fuss. I injured myself in the course of my inquiries. A first-aider cleaned it up and disinfected it and bandaged it and gave me an anti-tetanus booster and ticked me off for cutting myself so carelessly. It's not worth mentioning."

"OK I won't mention it. I'm just glad it's all right."

"And I'm glad you're all right."

"Myra and Oscar were there, weren't they?"

"Yes," he said. "They're both all right."

"Oh, good."

Then the nurse was at his shoulder. He bent over and kissed Sophie's cheek. She had closed her eyes. Probably she was already asleep. He tiptoed out, and went home.

After soaking for half an hour in a hot bath he sat by the Aga with a hot toddy and began to explore the possibilities.

By the time the glass was half empty the scales had fallen from his eyes and he knew he had found the killer of Gurth Tancred. It wasn't, after all, William Parchment. William had been lying all along but he hadn't been lying for himself; he had been lying for Ann Prideaux.

Suppose Ann Prideaux had gone to the lane to wait for Gurth. Suppose she was worried about his failed operations, worried for him and worried for the patients and, even more, perhaps, worried for William who was showing signs of being disturbed and of committing some rash act. Supposing she tackled Gurth and begged him to go away and dry out, and supposing he reacted, as most incipient alcoholics would, by indignantly denying that there was any problem.

Ann had been in a state of deep depression for weeks after the break-up of her affair with Gurth Tancred. She must have been brooding on that and on William's problems and probably on the Hay case, which seemed to have caused distress and anxiety to so many members of the hospital staff.

He saw then that he had so concentrated on William Parchment that he hadn't given any thought at all to Ann Prideaux. Supposing William had hidden, not his own shoes, but Ann's, in the Jacksons' freezer. If so, the answers on that would soon be available from the lab. She couldn't have taken the plastic mac to William to hide as she would have had to walk back through the lane and the hospital carrying a bloodstained mac and getting very wet. She would climb over the fence and hide the mac, probably in the hollow tree. Later she or William could have gone back, to cut up the mac and hide it in the coach house, cutting off the seams and buttons and leaving them in the tree.

It was only after murder had been done that the tickets for Australia had been booked, ostensibly to give William a rest. The true purpose of that trip could have been to get Ann away.

What motive could she have had? It couldn't, surely, have been premeditated. Was Ann Prideaux capable of beating the professor over the head with a heavy piece of wood? He would never have thought so. But his time in the CID had taught him that it's almost always difficult to imagine the murderer actually doing the deed even if you have incontrovertible proof that he did. And that where, as in the case of Oscar Hay, you allow yourself to pick out one person as a likely murderer, you prove almost always to be entirely wrong. In most cases, the outward appearance and the normal every-day behaviour give no clue whatsoever to the capacity for violence of any human being.

He looked at his watch. Still a few hours to spare. He'd been barking up any number of wrong trees but now he was on the right track. And never for one moment had he considered Ann Prideaux as a suspect.

There was absolutely no good reason why he should have been so sure that she didn't come into it. The only explanation for his stupidity was the involvement of

Sophie which had caused him to rush through the inquiry like a knife through butter.

Never mind. He'd done it in time for the deadline.

He threw on some clothes and went in search of the answers about the shoes. Then they would have to find where Ann Prideaux slept and take her into custody, having made sure that it checked out that the sneakers were hers.

33

Godfrey Baldwin

JOHN went back to Rope Walk. At 7.30 a.m. he left a message for Clarissa in the kitchen telling her he'd be bringing Sophie home very soon and asking her to keep Robert home from school. By 7.45 he was with Godfrey Baldwin for their third and last meeting on the Tancred case.

"Well, John?"

"We've done it, sir."

"And got Sophie safely back?"

"Yes. Sophie will soon be safe and sound at Mill House with the children."

"And you've got your murderer?"

"Yes, sir."

"In forty-eight hours. Not bad, John. Not bad at all."

"Thank you, sir. It's taken years off my life but we got there. It was the girlfriend of the surgical registrar, who happens to be the young pathologist who helped me out on the Hardcastle case. She's an unlucky girl. She'd had a bit of a fling with the murderer in that case and she'd had a bit of a fling with the victim in this one. It's ironic. The boyfriend was high on my list and that completely blinded me to the possibility that it was she. Said he had done it because he wanted to protect Ann. And of course that's why Sophie ran off. She knew that if he'd done it it was to stop Gurth Tancred harming the patients by operating when he was under the influence. She didn't want to have to testify against him and she knew she couldn't lie successfully to me. So she went to ground in Hartley Godwin's flat until they were safely airborne, bound for Australia. Ann Prideaux was worried about William's state of mind and thought she'd tackle Tancred before he did. Probably felt he would listen to her."

"With a good advocate and that background she may get away with a short sentence."

"I hope so. It's tricky. I don't see how you'd prove the *mens rea* in this case. Did she mean to kill him or did she simply hit out at him in blind fury and despair partly because she was afraid her boyfriend would go for him? It's complicated by the fact that she'd had an affair with the victim. That won't help. Parchment swore she'd given the professor the push. The Nursing Officer said it was the other way round. Who can tell which is true? She'll come over well in court. She's very composed but she has a gentle way with her. She sat there and lied in her teeth to me about the operation on the Hay child and the whole subject of Tancred's drinking. Parchment wanted to stop him operating. He knew about Hay's failed attempts to stop the man and he knew the little girl who died and felt very emotional about the whole thing, so, to turn my attention away from that, Ann told me there was no problem — that Tancred was unassailable on the competence of his operations. A bare-faced lie. She knew perfectly well that his colleagues were dead worried about his drinking. But in fact none of them did a thing about it except William. I've got a soft spot for that young man because of it. I hope he gets away with the accessory charge. There are strong mitigating factors."

"Don't worry about either of them. The medics will take care of them. They'll have the best possible advice."

"It's ironic that I thought Ann was arranging the trip to Australia to get William away whereas in fact he arranged it to get Ann away."

"Not very well done to try to implicate the hospital administrator and his wife by unloading the shoes on them."

"He probably didn't think it could get them arrested. He was just clouding the issue and getting shot of the evidence against Ann."

"They were her shoes?"

"Yes. Bob Jackson was high on the list of my suspects right up until the end. But William Parchment was always the most likely. The Secretary of State has a lot to answer for. He was worked into the ground and frantic with worry because the professor was likely to damage patients and no one seemed to care or to be ready to do anything about it. Oscar Hay had tried legal methods and met with a stone wall on every side.

"The unfortunate thing is that, if they'd consulted Harvey Knott, the pathologist, a regular old-fashioned medical man with common sense, he'd have solved the whole problem for them. Sent the man off to Switzerland for a prolonged holiday and cure, presented to him as the only alternative to the sack. They'd probably have sent his wife with him and they might have had a good time together for the first time in years. He'd have come back a wiser and perhaps a happier man. As it was no one did a thing and Ann Prideaux got so worried and mixed up about it that she had a brainstorm and hit him over the head. It seems he was one of those individuals with a fragile skull so that may help her. The ferocity of the blow was one of the nastiest aspects of the affair at first sight. As it is it seems that it may not have been a vicious blow. Poor girl. No wonder she was distraught that evening."

"Sad business. Let me have your report as soon as possible and I'll talk to the Chief Constable and the Commissioner. They ought to be satisfied. You've the luck of Old Nick, John! This could have finished you for good."

"Don't think I don't know it, sir. I'm tremendously grateful to you."

The phone rang and the ACC handed it to Charter.

"Your sergeant," he said.

"Sir," said Cobbold, "you were right. I found out where he lived. It's up at the caravan site on the Fillingham road. I went over there and interviewed him. He swore he'd no idea where Silke was. He'd been out with her once or twice but she wasn't his girlfriend. She wasn't in the caravan then but she must have sneaked in at the back during the night. I parked where I could keep them under obbo, and at 7 a.m. out they came together hand in hand. They didn't half get a surprise. He swore like a trooper and I'm rather glad I don't know German as I don't like to hear profanity from a young girl. Anyway they're both here at the station looking glum."

"Well done," said Charter. "I'll be straight over. There have been lively doings in the night, Sergeant, and you'll be glad to know that we've nailed our murderer. No, not Parchment. I'm afraid it's Ann Prideaux."

He turned to the ACC. "No further murder inquiry, sir. Sergeant Cobbold has unearthed Silke von Treiben. She was with the boyfriend up at the caravan site. They're at the station now."

"Satisfactory," said the ACC. "Good man, that sergeant of yours. Well go on, then. Go and get Sophie. Give her my good wishes and tell her to take care of herself and then to try and behave."

34

Back to Square One

AS he walked out of the hospital with Sophie they ran into Oscar and Mary Hay arm in arm, heading for the green MG. Hay came striding over to take his hand and pump it unmercifully up and down.

"Congratulations!" he said. "It was brilliant. And, of course, when I'd talked to Mary and knew that you'd hoisted it in about my neurosis on the subject of the sight of blood I understood what that little scene in the House was all about. At the time I was bewildered. When Mary told me about your conversation with her I saw at once that you had to have proof that I couldn't have delivered that blow without passing out myself. I knew you hadn't any time to waste and I must say I admire your guts. It's the sort of thing I'd do myself all things being equal. I always thought it was Parchment. Well, he'd told Sophie he'd done it and she told me. I thought he'd done it for the sake of the patients. I wasn't going to shop him for it. Anyway it's all over now."

"And I'm very grateful to you," said Mary Hay holding out her hand. "And I'm glad you're safe," she said to Sophie, and leaned forward to kiss her cheek.

Charter felt slightly guilty at the loathing he felt for Hay but he smiled at both of them and Sophie, to his relief, seemed quite pleased with Mary Hay's advances. They parted with smiles and waves and he put Sophie into his car and took her to Rope Walk.

"We'll collect the children and Cathy," he said, "and take them back to Mill House. Clarissa's still there and Bumble's had her kittens."

"And Flymo too?"

"Yes, Flymo's there too."

"I hope he hasn't eaten the kittens."

He hadn't. They all drove back to Mill House where they had a huge second breakfast and then put Sophie to bed.

It was twenty-four hours later that she came to see him at Rope Walk

301

and, looking at her sitting by his Aga drinking coffee, rosy-cheeked and smiling, he was reassured that she was perfectly recovered. Sophie had always been extremely resilient.

"It was you, wasn't it," he said, "in Mill House that night? I suppose you had to make sure I didn't get all that information about what was going on in the hospital."

"Yes," she said, "I'm sorry, John. That folder would have put you on to William and I was quite sure he had done it. He used to tell me how worried he was about Gurth. He kept saying 'I could kill him'."

"Yes, I expect he was saying the same thing to Ann Prideaux."

"John," said Sophie, "what I really don't understand is how did you know Myra wasn't really homicidal? I mean you said William told you Ann had seen her lying in wait for Gurth."

"That's what told me it wasn't Myra."

"How?"

"Because it wasn't true. He had obviously made that story up. And that told me it was either him or Ann Prideaux."

"How do you make that out?"

"Well, first of all, Ann Prideaux 'forgot' to tell me that she had been in the lane on the night of the murder. I learned elsewhere that she'd taken some notes over to Jackie Fisher. Secondly, William asked me to believe that Ann had completely forgotten seeing Myra lurking in the lane before the murder. I simply didn't believe it. So convenient a memory. Of course she would have remembered it if it were true. He saw I didn't quite swallow it so he then said the reason she remembered it this evening was that she'd seen Myra outside her house again in her dressing-gown and holding a knife. Now that I did believe. And that's why I ran, the minute I heard it. I knew she'd been given a very strong dose of some drug to quieten her down and she could be in a very confused state. I did believe that Ann had seen her and told William and that could have given him the idea of telling me that Ann had seen Myra in the lane on the night of the murder. He was getting very rattled by then."

"That's disgustingly clever of you."

"Not really. I'd just discovered that William had the opportunity to put the shoes where we found them in the Jackson kitchen. They are Ann Prideaux's shoes. She admitted it. And they fit the print the murderer left in the lane."

"Myra's being kept in for a day or two," Sophie told him. "I took her some flowers and the room's like a florist's shop. She's holding court in there with Mrs Harvey Knott. She's loving it. You'd better go in and see her. She wants to thank you. She says she's very sorry for Ann Prideaux and for William. I wouldn't be surprised if she decides to visit them in jail. And now I must dash. I've a thousand things to do."

"Are you all right at Mill House?"

"Yes of course we are. Why?"

"I just wondered if things were getting a bit expensive with inflation and now Robert's at school. Can you manage on the money?"

"Of course I can. I know how much you earn, John. In fact you're bloody generous and I've always said so to everybody."

"Don't."

"Don't what?"

"Don't talk to everybody about our private arrangements."

"I don't."

"But you've just said — "

"Oh stop it, John. I don't want to fight with you. Just this once let's not argue."

"Very well." He walked over and kissed her on the mouth. "Go home, Sophie. I've got to work."

For once she leaned up and kissed him back.

"Very well, John," she said. "You're a marvel, you know. I can't think why you put up with me."

She left him on the doorstep gazing after her with a bemused look on his face and, as she got into her car, she looked back at him, still standing there looking thunderstruck, and Sophie suddenly laughed at him quite freely and spontaneously, like a child.

"Come back," he called, opening his arms wide but she shook her head, waved a hand and drove away.

THE WILDERNESS WALK
Sheila Bishop

Stifling unpleasant memories of a misbegotten romance in Cleave with Lord Francis Aubrey, Lavinia goes on holiday there with her sister. The two women are thrust into a romantic intrigue involving none other than Lord Francis.

THE RELUCTANT GUEST
Rosalind Brett

Ann Calvert went to spend a month on a South African farm with Theo Borland and his sister. They both proved to be different from her first idea of them, and there was Storr Peterson — the most disturbing man she had ever met.

ONE ENCHANTED SUMMER
Anne Tedlock Brooks

A tale of mystery and romance and a girl who found both during one enchanted summer.

CLOUD OVER MALVERTON
Nancy Buckingham

Dulcie soon realises that something is seriously wrong at Malverton, and when violence strikes she is horrified to find herself under suspicion of murder.

AFTER THOUGHTS
Max Bygraves

The Cockney entertainer tells stories of his East End childhood, of his RAF days, and his post-war showbusiness successes and friendships with fellow comedians.

MOONLIGHT AND MARCH ROSES
D. Y. Cameron

Lynn's search to trace a missing girl takes her to Spain, where she meets Clive Hendon. While untangling the situation, she untangles her emotions and decides on her own future.

NURSE ALICE IN LOVE
Theresa Charles

Accepting the post of nurse to little Fernie Sherrod, Alice Everton could not guess at the romance, suspense and danger which lay ahead at the Sherrod's isolated estate.

POIROT INVESTIGATES
Agatha Christie

Two things bind these eleven stories together — the brilliance and uncanny skill of the diminutive Belgian detective, and the stupidity of his Watson-like partner, Captain Hastings.

LET LOOSE THE TIGERS
Josephine Cox

Queenie promised to find the long-lost son of the frail, elderly murderess, Hannah Jason. But her enquiries threatened to unlock the cage where crucial secrets had long been held captive.

THE TWILIGHT MAN
Frank Gruber

Jim Rand lives alone in the California desert awaiting death. Into his hermit existence comes a teenage girl who blows both his past and his brief future wide open.

DOG IN THE DARK
Gerald Hammond

Jim Cunningham breeds and trains gun dogs, and his antagonism towards the devotees of show spaniels earns him many enemies. So when one of them is found murdered, the police are on his doorstep within hours.

THE RED KNIGHT
Geoffrey Moxon

When he finds himself a pawn on the chessboard of international espionage with his family in constant danger, Guy Trent becomes embroiled in moves and countermoves which may mean life or death for Western scientists.

TIGER TIGER
Frank Ryan

A young man involved in drugs is found murdered. This is the first event which will draw Detective Inspector Sandy Woodings into a whirlpool of murder and deceit.

CAROLINE MINUSCULE
Andrew Taylor

Caroline Minuscule, a medieval script, is the first clue to the whereabouts of a cache of diamonds. The search becomes a deadly kind of fairy story in which several murders have an other-worldly quality.

LONG CHAIN OF DEATH
Sarah Wolf

During the Second World War four American teenagers from the same town join the Army together. Forty-two years later, the son of one of the soldiers realises that someone is systematically wiping out the families of the four men.

THE LISTERDALE MYSTERY
Agatha Christie

Twelve short stories ranging from the light-hearted to the macabre, diverse mysteries ingeniously and plausibly contrived and convincingly unravelled.

TO BE LOVED
Lynne Collins

Andrew married the woman he had always loved despite the knowledge that Sarah married him for reasons of her own. So much heartache could have been avoided if only he had known how vital it was to be loved.

ACCUSED NURSE
Jane Converse

Paula found herself accused of a crime which could cost her her job, her nurse's reputation, and even the man she loved, unless the truth came to light.

BUTTERFLY MONTANE
Dorothy Cork

Parma had come to New Guinea to marry Alec Rivers, but she found him completely disinterested and that overbearing Pierce Adams getting entirely the wrong idea about her.

HONOURABLE FRIENDS
Janet Daley

Priscilla Burford is happily married when she meets Junior Environment Minister Alistair Thurston. Inevitably, sexual obsession and political necessity collide.

WANDERING MINSTRELS
Mary Delorme

Stella Wade's career as a concert pianist might have been ruined by the rudeness of a famous conductor, so it seemed to her agent and benefactor. Even Sir Nicholas fails to see the possibilities when John Tallis falls deeply in love with Stella.

MORNING IS BREAKING
Lesley Denny

The growing frenzy of war catapults Diane Clements into a clandestine marriage and separation with a German refugee.

LAST BUS TO WOODSTOCK
Colin Dexter

A girl's body is discovered huddled in the courtyard of a Woodstock pub, and Detective Chief Inspector Morse and Sergeant Lewis are hunting a rapist and a murderer.

THE STUBBORN TIDE
Anne Durham

Everyone advised Carol not to grieve so excessively over her cousin's death. She might have followed their advice if the man she loved thought that way about her, but another girl came first in his affections.